GW00494555

MANHUNT

ON A MANHUNT - BOOK 1

VANESSA VALE

Manhunt by Vanessa Vale

Copyright © 2022 by Bridger Media

This is a work of fiction. Names, characters, places and incidents are the products of the author's imagination and used fictitiously. Any resemblance to actual persons, living or dead, businesses, companies, events or locales is entirely coincidental.

All rights reserved.

No part of this book may be reproduced in any form or by any electronic or mechanical means, including information storage and retrieval systems, without written permission from both authors, except for the use of brief quotations in a book review.

Cover design: Sarah Hansen/Okay Creations

Cover graphic: Marishiav/Shutterstock

1

BRIDGET

Friday 6:05 pm

THE LAST THING I wanted to do at work on a Friday at six was fill out a sex quiz.

On a scale of 1 to 10, how kinky you are?

I glanced at the question on my computer screen and rolled my eyes. Then they snagged on the time in the upper right corner, and I panicked.

"Fuck. I don't have time for this," I muttered to myself. I hadn't finished updating the graph on my desk in front of me or adjusted the project schedule or any of the other things that got pushed back because of the meeting earlier. Just like everything else on the James Inn build. Instead, I rushed to finally fill out a silly sex quiz my BFF was forcing me to complete.

It was after six and no one else was in the office, the others having cut out for the weekend already. It wasn't that I was more diligent, but I was dreading going to happy hour.

Yeah, that was me. The weird woman who didn't want to meet up with her bestie and others for ladies' night. I liked my friends, but the friends were bringing friends and the bar would be crowded. Men on the prowl. Ladies on a manhunt. I wasn't interested. It made me nervous. Uncomfortable.

And I *really* didn't want to have my quiz shared, like all of them would. My sex life sucked, and I didn't need to share it.

I typed my answer about being kinky with "No comment" then scanned the next question.

If you didn't answer, is it because you are a virgin?

"Jesus." I couldn't believe Mallory had come up with this. No, I could. It was just like her to be so bold and... insane. To take something from an eighties movie and put a modern–and adult–spin on it.

I jammed the N and the O keys extra hard.

How many partners have you had?

My cell rang and I jumped, then when I saw the display, I grabbed it up and answered. "I can't believe you're making me take this stupid quiz," I told my best friend instead of hello.

"I can't believe you haven't answered any of my calls," Mallory countered, but wouldn't be distracted. "And the quiz is for ladies' night."

That, I already knew. She'd been pestering me about it for almost a week. Yes, I'd been holding off that long. As for ignoring her, I'd seen she'd called three times and left four texts, but it'd been too crazy to reply.

"I had to hear from Jemma about the gorgeous man in your office."

Of course Mallory would get the latest from Jemma, the office manager, who she knew since she came to the office sometimes.

"I want to hear alllllll about it."

"Sex quiz or details on Maverick James?" I offered her the options, but I wasn't sure which one she was going to pick.

"Shit, that's a tough call. It's going to be so much fun reading all the sex quiz answers," she replied with enthusiasm that bordered on giddy. "But from what I heard from Jemma, a woman can orgasm by the sound of that man's voice."

That wasn't too far from the truth.

"I hate you," I growled, playing with my ponytail and remembering I had a pencil behind my ear. I tossed it onto my desk.

"What's got your panties in a twist? What's wrong with being horny for the hot boss?"

I rested my forehead in my hand and shook my head.

"It's been a day," I explained, leaving out the fact that a lot of my frustration really did have to do with the guy. My boss's boss. The hot one. Who I really was horny for. Not that I would admit that to Mallory. She'd make me go shopping and wear makeup to work for him to notice me.

I'd done that all by myself earlier. No makeup needed.

"Tell me *all* about it," she continued on a sigh. "Especially if it involves Maverick James, that gorgeous piece of man meat."

"How do you know–"

"I looked him up online after I talked to Jemma."

Of course she had. She wasn't lying about him, except– "If you want me to get to the bar on time, or anytime tonight, I need to finish the quiz."

It was the only way I could think of to get her to

stop talking about him. Talk about a guy making me nervous and uncomfortable.

She and I had watched the *Sixteen Candles* movie two weeks ago and she decided that making a sex quiz–like in the movie–and sharing answers tonight with a bunch of girlfriends was happening.

"You haven't finished it yet? Don't tell me you're still at work."

"Fine, I won't tell you."

Another sigh came through the phone. "You need to take that Physics teacher job at the high school. You'd have your summer off like me."

"Not all of us can teach first grade," I countered.

"Whatever. I thought you were going to go home and change into the cute top."

The cute top she was talking about was hanging in the back of my closet and never to appear. It was banished there as Mallory forced me to order it. It wasn't something I ever planned on wearing. Not that it was over-the-top or inappropriate, it just wasn't me. Or, it showed too much of *me.* I glanced down at myself. Jeans and a long-sleeved white t-shirt. Plain. Boring.

"The project is behind schedule," I told her instead of continuing the conversation about why I didn't want to wear *the cute top.* I was content being less seen.

Blending in. The clusterfuck earlier today was an example of that. Being a woman on a huge construction site was bad enough. I didn't want to look... good. I wanted to work and get on with my unexciting little life. "Besides the coffee spill, the framers are going to add a second crew," I continued, pushing the point home that things were hectic. "The electrical team is on hold until next Thursday and my boss got fired."

"Maverick James was fired?" she screeched.

Out of all the issues, she focused on that. "Not him. He's the owner, remember. Maverick *James* as in James Corporation. My boss's boss."

"So your boss's boss fired your boss?"

That had been a scene and I curled in on myself even remembering. I didn't like confrontations and that had been a doozy. And about me. "Yes."

"Good. That guy is a total sleaze."

In the past, I'd shared with her how much of a dick the guy was. I was going to have a drink–or two–later to celebrate his departure and the spectacular way it was done.

"I'll see you in a few at Kincaid's," I told her.

"Hell no," she replied. I imagined her holding her hand up in front of her. "I'm not letting you off the phone until you finish the quiz and email it to me. Then you'll drive your butt right to over here to the bar."

I rolled my eyes at the ceiling, then back to the screen. "Fine."

I set the cell to speaker mode and sat it on my desk so I could type with two hands.

To the number of partners question, I typed in 1.

It was a sad number at twenty-two and my prospects to change it weren't on the horizon.

What's the one thing you wish you got from your partners?

That was easy. Orgasms.

"I hear the keyboard clacking. I hope that means you're doing the quiz and not some fancy math validating the vertical structural integrity of an I-beam."

"Vertical structural integrity?" I asked, my fingers stilling. "What does that even mean?"

"I have no idea. You're the math and engineering brainiac."

I sighed, trying to keep up with Mallory's busy thoughts. I was the quiet shy one and she was the extrovert constantly trying to pull me out of my shell. It had worked since elementary school when our desks were side by side, but after high school, I'd gone to MIT for college. Far from Hunter Valley, Montana. When everyone wanted to know why I'd returned a semester early and without my degree, it hadn't helped. Mallory was trying, but it was going to take more than a sex quiz and ladies' night to get me out there again. "Do you want me to finish this quiz or not?"

"Finish. Finish. Finish," she began to chant.

I laughed, then pushed on.

What do you want a guy to do to you in bed? This is anonymous so share your darkest fantasy.

I exhaled loudly.

"You're on the fantasy question, aren't you?"

"Yup." I paused, stared at the blinking cursor, then typed. What the hell, I thought. It was anonymous since no name was on top and Mallory was going to print them all out and bring the stack to the bar. Knowing the other ladies who were joining us and answered their own sex quizzes, my fantasy response would sound like it came from a nun in comparison. They weren't tramps or anything. Not that any woman was a tramp, but these were more Mallory's friends than mine since I'd been gone for three years and I always felt like I was tagging along. I may have left the time zone, but I was back now. Home with my proverbial tail between my legs.

"What does it matter? I mean, guys go for pretty women like you and your friends. High maintenance.

Like you said, I'm just the smart one not wearing the cute top."

"Bridget Jane Morrison, we need to find a man who will spank your ass for me for saying that."

My mouth fell open. "I can't believe you just said that."

"I can't believe you just put yourself down. *Again.*"

I frowned, then typed in my answer. My secret fantasy.

Moving on... *Who do you want to do it with? Name your dream lay.*

"Bridge, come on. What the hell's taking so long?" she poked.

I typed in the first thing that came to mind to get this over with and Mallory off my back. Jake Ryan. The cute hero from *Sixteen Candles.* The same answer that Samantha gave in the movie. My first true–fictional–love.

"Done," I say, saving the document.

"Send it and let's go already. I'm wearing that new push up bra and I have to tell you my girls never looked so perky."

Mallory regaled me all about the benefits of her new bra as if she worked with structural engineers instead of me. She moved on to making the Jeopardy countdown music which was as annoying as someone filing their nails in front of you as I attached the document and hit Send.

"Done!" I shouted, hoping she stopped.

"Finally. See you in a few. And don't get side-tracked by some report. I will hunt you down!" She hung up.

Hopping up, I grabbed my things and headed out, ensuring the office's entry door was locked. Climbing into my car, I slumped in my seat and took a breath. Friday night. Thank God. I didn't hate my job, but there were aspects of it that sucked. Like my boss. Now my ex-boss. The letch. I didn't want to think about him now, or ever, again. I shifted my thoughts to my latest and greatest fantasy instead and put all my mental power on my ride across town to Maverick James.

Big. Manly. Hot. Brash. And I didn't realize until earlier today, a badass. A gorgeous, older badass. Broad shoulders. Muscular like exercise was his religion. Square jaw. Dark, penetrating eyes that didn't just look at you, but into you and made you squirm.

I did just that now in my car thinking of him. My panties didn't stand a chance when he was around. Or on my mind.

Ten minutes later, I searched the interior of Kincaid's for Mallory and the others. Happy hour was in full swing and the crowd spilled out onto an exterior deck.

"You're not going to get away with it," Mallory said, setting her hands on my shoulders once I found the group at two high top tables pushed together out on the deck. Her blue gaze raked me over as she spoke. She shook her head, and I knew she was taking in my outfit. "Are those boots even sold in women's sizes?"

Of course she looked adorable in a pair of high waisted jeans and pale blue, low cut top that only validated everything she said about the push-up bra. Her light hair was styled and she had on makeup. Like a normal twenty-something on a Friday night.

"Getting away with what? My shoes?" I glanced down at my feet. "It's a law that I have to wear steel toed shoes at a construction site."

"Not the shoes, although they are God-awful. Leave a pair of non-construction site shoes in your car or something. I'm talking about the quiz."

I frowned as I waved to Zoe, one of Mallory's friends, over her shoulder. "What are you talking about?"

"You didn't send it."

I blinked at her. "Yes, I did."

She shook her head, her hair swinging along with

cute, dangly earrings. I reached up and felt the tiny stud in my ear.

"Well, I didn't get it," she said, sounding put off.

My eyes widened as I felt a trickle of panic. "What do you mean you didn't get it?"

She held up her phone and I grabbed her wrist so I could see her inbox on the screen. "I. Didn't. Get. It."

My mind started to spin, wondering where it did go. I stared at Mallory. She stared at me.

"If it didn't go to you, then where did I send it?"

I grabbed my cell from my crossbody purse and opened up my own email. Swiped to the Sent folder and—

Screamed.

Right there in the middle of Kincaid's, like I was trying out for a horror flick.

All talking on the deck ceased and everyone turned to face me. I didn't pay them any attention. All my focus was on the name in the To section of my email along with the attachment titled *Sex Quiz.*

"Oh my God." My heart was trying to beat right out of my chest and my hands shook.

Mallory snagged the phone from my hand as I willed the ground to open up and swallow me down. A single-person sinkhole would be perfect.

"Holy shit," she whispered, eyes widening, then meeting mine. "How did that happen?"

Since I didn't seem to be actually dying, the bar patrons went back to their fun while I was going to have a stroke or expire of mortification.

I grabbed the cell back, stared at it, willing my eyes to be wrong. "You're Mallory. He's Maverick. They both start with the same two letters. M. A. You were doing that annoying *Jeopardy* music and it must have auto-filled the rest of the address and I wasn't paying any attention."

"With your boss's boss's name."

I nodded, trying not to vomit because she didn't know everything that happened today. "Mal, I just sent a sex quiz to Maverick James."

2

MAVERICK

FRIDAY 10:18 am - Eight hours before the scream

THE LAST THING I expected this week was to be in Montana. Since the project in Hunter Valley wasn't going smoothly–meaning it was somehow ridiculously over budget and behind schedule, I had my assistant rearrange my appointments for me to be here. It had been my idea to convert a local ranch property into a posh inn. To shift the development of our corporate chain of hotels from large mega-properties like on the Las Vegas Strip, New York's Fifth Avenue or Belgravia in London to exclusive destinations with only a handful of guests. These new additions offered top amenities with unusual and custom excursions.

The first one in the San Juan Islands in Washington State had a waitlist after only being open three months. The latest in Banff opened last month. The project here in Hunter Valley was the third and while I'd been monitoring it closely, I doubted it was going to be ready for prime ski season. Not with the long list of issues.

That wasn't going to work. I'd had enough excuses and cost overrides from the project manager. Not for me and not for the board of directors who'd backed me.

I flew up here to get it back on schedule and figure out what the hell was going on.

While it was my family's last name on the side of the corporate headquarters in Denver, it was my ass and personal reputation at stake. I was CEO and it was my–and my brother Silas's–company. I didn't like to fail, and it wasn't going to start now.

The jet landed an hour ago and my first stop in town was for coffee. I'd driven down the quaint Main Street, found Steaming Hotties, which was one hell of a name for a coffee shop, and parked out front. I took in the exposed brick walls, high-beamed ceilings inside. Eclectic tables and chairs were filled with even more eclectic customers ranging from old-timers in overalls to two moms wrangling toddlers with chocolate mustaches and crumbling muffins in their little fists.

The scent of coffee made me start to perk up. This wasn't the twenty-third floor of James Corp. This right here, this caffeine and sugar scented business, was a reason why I chose this valley for the resort. It was like a break from the real world without any big chain stores or restaurants. It was near the state's national parks, but off the beaten path to have too many tourists. A ski resort was nestled in the mountains at the edge of town, meaning the valley offered both summer and winter activities. I'd skied here a number of times and knew from those visits this town would be on the list for one of my boutique inns.

This town was calm. Quaint. Easy going.

Friendly, too, based on the big smile and welcome from the barista. "Hey there! What can I get you today?"

"Coffee, black. To go." I glanced at the bakery case. "Are those cinnamon rolls homemade?"

She smiled. "Sure are."

My stomach rumbled. "One of those."

"Good call. Want it warmed up? It'll be better that way."

"Sounds good. Thanks."

I leaned against the counter as she began to fill my order, checking emails on my cell.

"No, something's off with that calculation. The length and width of the space is what?"

The soft voice had me glancing over my shoulder. A woman was on the phone, papers tucked under her arm. She had glasses on her nose, dark hair pulled into a somewhat sloppy ponytail.

The barista handed me my to-go cup and I passed her some cash as she said, "I'll let you know when the cinnamon roll is ready."

"Eight seven by twenty-nine point five," the woman behind me said. "Right."

I stuffed the change I was given into a vintage tea pot serving as a tip jar, grabbed my coffee and made my way over to the napkin dispenser at the milk and sugar station. If the cinnamon roll was as gooey and frosting covered as it looked in the case, I was going to need several.

"That's... twenty-five sixty-six and a half for square footage," the woman continued.

Wait, did she do that math in her head? I glanced

to see if she was reading something on those papers. Nope. They were still stuffed beneath her arm.

She bit her lip, clearly thinking. While her gaze was on the list of coffee drinks on the chalkboard on the brick wall behind the counter, she wasn't seeing any of it. "Doesn't the report say twenty-eight something?"

I started listening more intently to her half of the conversation. I grabbed a stir stick to look busy with my coffee, even though I liked it black, and not like I was eavesdropping. I had no idea what she was talking about, but I was fascinated. Whatever the math problem, she wasn't using a calculator or one in her cell phone.

"Hey Bridge. Usual?" the barista asked.

Bridge. An odd name.

She–Bridge–moved the phone away from her head as she answered. "You got it. Thanks, Eve."

Bridge moved to a high top beneath the large picture window looking out onto the street, set her papers down with a sigh. "That's one of the problems," she continued with whomever was on the call. "The math's way off. They're overcharging by over two hundred square feet. Yes, I'm sure."

She tipped her head up at the tin ceiling and while I could only see her back, I knew she was probably rolling her eyes. I had to smile. "Yes, I understand you have to check my math. Pull out your calculator and see. I'll wait."

As she did that, she glanced around the shop and her gaze snagged on me. Her mouth dropped open and her eyes widened. I was used to the reaction. I was a big guy. Around here, all I was missing was a flannel shirt and an ax to be considered a lumberjack.

I reached for a napkin and tugged it from the dispenser.

What I hadn't noticed the first time her eyes met mine was that they were green. Like emeralds, fringed by dark lashes and only magnified by her glasses. She pushed them up her nose and I found the action strangely endearing, right along with the pencil tucked behind her ear. She was a tiny thing, maybe an inch or two over five feet. Just a little peanut in comparison to me.

And young. Early twenties, I guessed, which was practically robbing the cradle since I was pushing forty. Fuck, I felt old. Maybe she was in college and working on some group project.

Shit. Was I eyeing a college coed?

Unlike most women I was used to who wore perfectly fitted dresses or suits at corporate, or even tighter yoga pants and snug tops out and about, this half pint had on loose fitting jeans and a simple long-sleeved shirt.

Not one part of her caught my eye. At first.

But now, with a second and third glance, every-thing about her was intriguing. Worth another look, which I took. Those jeans couldn't hide rounded hips or a perfect ass and while her top was simple, the swell of pert breasts was enough to make me need to wipe drool with the napkin I held.

When she realized she was staring–even though I was staring right back–she blushed and looked away, shifted her gaze to the worn wood flooring and her work boot-covered feet.

On top of all that about her, she was shy. Definitely not trying to catch my interest. My smile grew at her... naturalness. Was that even a fucking word? I had no idea but that was this woman.

Young. Pretty.

Great. She was exactly what my father used to like and that made me feel like shit for even looking her way. The last thing I wanted was to be anything like him.

"Yes, I'm still here. Yes." She spun back to the table, her ponytail whipping around her neck, clearly flus-tered. I knew I was reasonably good looking and fit, but my size was intimidating.

I was, at thirty-seven, still very single. After all these years, that meant I wasn't much of a catch to anyone who wasn't a money-hungry bitch. I steered well clear of those.

Who was this woman and why was I curious about her? Why was I suddenly interested in learning more about her?

I pulled out another napkin.

"That was my math, too," she continued. "Yes. I'm glad the discrepancy was found."

The barista held up a glass of iced coffee to catch her attention, then to me with the cinnamon roll big and gooey enough to fill the plate it sat on.

"Look, I have to go," she said. "The meeting's this afternoon. Yes, I'll have all the data ready."

She ended the call, set her cell on the table beside her papers and went to the counter.

"Problems?" the barista–Eve–asked her.

Bridge shrugged as I stepped up behind her to get my cinnamon roll. "Nothing more than usual. Just a big meeting later and problems to solve."

"They're lucky to have you and that big brain of yours," Eve said sweetly. It was clear they knew each other. Close in age, too. Probably grew up together.

Bridge smiled and paid for her drink. "You're

sweeter than your baked goods for saying that. And this brain's gotten me into nothing but trouble."

She tapped her temple as she spoke and spun on her heel and turned right into me. The glass of iced coffee hit my chest and splashed all over it.

I took a step back instinctively. She gasped.

"Shit, I'm so sorry!" she said, setting the now empty glass on the counter, then grabbed the napkins out of my grip.

She started to pat at my shirt to sop up the chilly coffee. I wore jeans with a dress shirt, my sleeves rolled up because even in Montana, it was a warm summer day. Now the white cotton had a huge swath of brown and it was dripping down my stomach. It was cold against my skin, but I barely felt it since Bridge's little hand was pressing over and over against my abs. Left, right, then moved lower.

And lower.

"I can't believe I did that." Her gaze didn't lift to mine as she tried to tackle the spill. "I'll pay for your dry cleaning and I–

I grabbed her wrist as she worked her way south toward the button on my jeans. A few inches lower and she'd be patting my dick. While I was all for her becoming acquainted with it, I didn't want that to happen here.

It seemed I needed more than an iced coffee bath to cool off from this woman's touch because I was getting hard.

I kept my hold gentle but needed to ensure she didn't work her way any lower. She was already freaked out enough. I might want to get better acquainted, but I liked the woman who touched my dick–or rode it–to know at least my name.

"Shh, it's okay," I murmured.

All I saw was the top of her head as she shook it. Her hair wasn't just brown but had hints of red and copper in it. I wondered how silky soft it would feel, how it would fall over her shoulders if I tugged out the tie.

"It's not. Your shirt's ruined," she practically moaned.

"Baby, look at me."

I had no idea where that endearment came from, but it fell from my lips as easily as the smile I offered her when she finally looked up, pencil behind her ear, her glasses perched on her nose and her hand clutching damp napkins. God, she was cute. I never knew I had a thing for nerdy twenty-somethings. No, not all of them, just this one in particular. Instantly, I wanted to reassure her, to make her see it wasn't anything to be upset about.

"It was an accident. I'm just glad you like iced coffee." I offered her a smile so she knew I wasn't upset, rubbed my thumb against her palm. I shouldn't be doing this... it was like robbing the fucking cradle just talking to her, but I couldn't help it.

Her eyes widened and she blinked. A flush spread across her cheeks. I didn't pull away. I couldn't.

"Still, I'm sorry. Your shirt's ruined, I'm sure," she whispered, glancing away, but not moving since I still held her.

"Eyes up here."

She responded immediately to my request, and I liked that. Too fucking much. I wondered how she'd respond when I took charge in other ways.

Oh shit. No. Not a good idea.

Fuck, yes.

"It's just a shirt," I said, my voice rough.

Eve came around the counter and handed me a clean dishcloth. I let go of Bridge to take it, but she snagged it out of her friend's hand before I could get it. She dropped to her knees to wipe up the floor. There wasn't much of a mess since it had landed squarely on me, and I was a big guy.

Bridge glanced up at me from her knees, sank her teeth in her plump lower lip and my dirty mind went immediately to her before me just like this, but I was feeding her my dick. How her lips would spread around it. How her eyes would go wide when she realized she wouldn't be able to take all of me.

I was at least a head taller and weighed close to two-fifty. Big. I was definitely proportionate. Shit. I was trying to be a good guy, a gentleman, but she was on her fucking knees! She was testing the hell out of my restraint and she didn't even know it.

Because it was fucking obvious she sure as shit was a good girl.

And I wanted to do very bad things to her. The very young woman. Now I could see why my dad liked them young.

I stifled a groan. I was going to hell.

I hadn't realized Eve had left us until she came back and handed me a t-shirt. "On the house."

The moment was broken, and I took the shirt, held it up. The coffee shop's name, Steaming Hotties, was across the chest in a decorative font with Hunter Valley, Montana beneath it. And it was pale pink.

"Might be a little snug," she added, "but I'm not sure what would fit on you, big guy."

I had my suitcase in the rental car. I could go out and grab a clean shirt, but it was a kind gesture, and I didn't want to decline it or her hospitality. Maybe I'd get her to supply the coffee beans for the inn. I might only be here a short time to get the construction project back on track, but I'd be in Hunter Valley often and wanted to get to know the community.

Perhaps one member of it in particular. One who seemed to be very talented at math, had a knack for blushing at the smallest things, was a touch awkward and didn't realize how amazing she looked on her knees.

On top of all that, I had a feeling the sooner I was out of the stained shirt, Bridge would stop looking at me like she kicked my puppy. I wanted her to look at me with those bewitching eyes in other ways. Ways that made me feel like an old fucking man. But one whose dick was rock hard.

So standing in the middle of the coffee shop, I took my shirt off, one button at a time.

3

BRIDGET

OH MY GOD. He was taking off his shirt. I'd never been to an all-male revue, but I had a feeling it would be like this. And I had a *very* up-close view. I hopped from my knees and Eve snagged the dirty cloth from my hands as I stared.

And tried not to drool as the man's bare chest was revealed, one chiseled inch at a time.

"Holy fuck," Eve whispered, then fled behind the counter to help another customer.

I had never seen a guy his size before. I worked on a construction site and was surrounded by men all day. Some were big, but not like this. I barely came up to this guy's shoulder. His wide, muscular shoulders. I knew they were muscular because they were bare. Bare! And tanned. And toned. And all the adjectives that were not coming to mind because I couldn't think straight at the sight of him.

And his thick chest. The smattering of dark hair. The flat disks of his nipples. I wanted to run my hand over one, then slide down over those abs. I stared and while I was one semester shy of getting a mathematics degree from MIT, I couldn't count if he had a six-, eight-, twelve-pack or whatever number he had if my life depended on it. His jeans hung low on his narrow hips and there were those two deep lines that dipped beneath the waistband, that V thing. The one that made a woman's ovaries pop out an egg or two.

He slipped his arms–yeah, they were corded and toned too–through the t-shirt and pulled it over his head, tugging it down over his body, where it barely fit.

"Eyes up here," he murmured, his voice deep and rumbly.

I flicked my gaze up to his instantly, just as I had the last time he'd said that to me, but I hadn't been entranced by the sliver of skin that was still exposed between the hem of the t-shirt and the top of his jeans. Now, it was hard to stare at anything else.

Gah!

I could feel my cheeks burning and I glanced quickly away, biting my lip. I'd been ogling him, like a huge slab of meat.

Long fingers lifted my chin back up.

The look in his dark eyes when mine met his didn't show anger. Little crinkles formed at the corners. He was smiling at me. Me!

The woman who'd–

"The spill," he said. "It's over. I got a cool new shirt out of it." He tugged at the cotton that stretched taut over his abs, at least a size too small. I doubted Eve carried lumberjack-size. The pink color only amplified his manliness.

His grin was lethal. So was the rest of him. Tanned, toned and totally hot. A giant.

He made my brain short circuit and I opened and closed my mouth a few times. "I–" I had no idea what to say.

He was trying to reassure me, which I wasn't used to. He was being nice. And he called me *baby*. Of course he called me an endearment. He didn't know my name.

It was probably how he kept all the women who threw themselves at him–or threw coffee on him–happy without having to remember their names. An easy way not to mess up. That made the most sense,

him calling every woman he encountered the same
thing.

"Sit with me?" he asked.

Sit with him? What?

"Come on." He snagged my hand in his big one
and pulled me over to the table where I abandoned
my work papers. I settled onto a stool and he sat across
from me, never letting go of my hand. His was like a
dinner plate, mine lost in his hold. The touch was
warm. Gentle. His fingers offered mine a small
squeeze.

I processed all this as I stared at it in his–his left
hand that didn't have a ring–then thought... HE'S
HOLDING MY HAND!

Chill, Bridge.

I pulled it away, tucked it into my lap so I didn't
reach out and run my fingers through his dark hair.
Threads of gray at the temples caught the sunlight
through the window, an indication he was older than
me. By a lot. Late thirties, probably.

"I'll be right back."

Before I could question what he meant, he took
three big steps and grabbed his coffee from the high
counter, then the plated cinnamon roll–with a fork
poked into the frosting–Eve held out for him. Her

smile was a little too big and a little too bright, proving that he could strike all women dumb.

Eve was my friend since 4H back in second grade. We knew each other well although I couldn't miss her response to him since she fanned herself behind his back. I totally agreed. He could melt any woman's hard drive.

"Work problems?" he asked once seated, eyes on my papers. They were an amalgamation of invoices, scribbled notes, jotted math workings and blueprint printouts.

So many problems. Like my dumbass boss, Jason, who couldn't use a calculator. That would involve work and he didn't like to do it. So as his assistant, I did it for him. When I started back in the winter, I'd just moved back and was desperate for a job.

"I figured it out," I replied neutrally. Unlike my inability to hold a glass of iced coffee, my job wasn't his problem. I didn't need to dump anything else on him.

"I heard you doing some math," he mentioned, pulling the fork from his cinnamon roll like he was Arthur pulling the sword from the cream cheese frosting covered stone.

I couldn't help but roll my eyes at his comment. I was used to being made fun of for what some considered a strange talent. Ever since I was little and advanced math couldn't challenge me. I considered it normal, although I was far from that. The nerdy girl. The brainiac. "Heard? My brain isn't that loud."

A slow smile crept across his face and my mind blanked. His good looks actually made me stupid.

"I'm impressed."

I shrugged and stood, not interested in being considered a sideshow for him. That happened to me enough without it being done by the most handsome man I'd ever seen. It was only even more insulting.

"It's just math." With a swipe of my hand, I corralled my papers. "I'll let you enjoy your coffee and roll."

"No. Stay." He hopped to his feet which had him looming over me once more. I swallowed hard at his command, and the earnestness behind it. "You never even got your drink."

Yeah, I didn't get it. He did. All over him.

He twisted and raised his arm to signal Eve, who somehow understood the hand gesture and held up a replacement iced coffee she'd already made, this time in a to-go cup.

He grabbed it from her and brought it to the table, setting it beside my papers. "There. Like nothing happened except I now get to have coffee with a beautiful woman."

My mouth fell open, then I snapped it shut and bit my lip to keep it that way.

Beautiful? Me? Right. I didn't dare look at him because I didn't want him to be a bullshitter. My sister, Lindy, always pointed out I could be beautiful if I put some effort in, and I knew I hadn't put any effort in this morning. Not with my boss always eyeing my ass. It was better–and smarter–to look as unfeminine as possible around him.

"Aren't you going to have some of your drink?" he asked, sitting back down. He cut off a section of cinnamon roll and ate it.

"I'm afraid to touch it and spill it on you again," I admitted, looking down.

I was afraid I would be clumsy, but not afraid in general. He didn't give off that vibe. In fact, he oddly felt... safe. I was also in a coffee shop in broad daylight with Eve as a chaperone. He seemed nice, except for the lie about me being beautiful. I couldn't figure out what he wanted from me for saying that.

I ran my hand over my hair absently and came across the pencil I'd tucked behind my ear.

God, soooo beautiful with my geeky pencil. I practically whimpered in mortification.

He set his fork on his plate so the tines faced down. "Did it ever occur to you that getting covered in coffee was just as much my fault? I stood right behind you."

I lifted my gaze and met his, surprised. What?

"I–"

He narrowed his eyes in such a way that had me snapping my mouth shut once more before I could argue.

"Drink your coffee, baby."

I took a sip of my drink. Why? To appease him? Because I was too stunned by the endearment again to do anything else?

"I... I really do have to get back to work," I told him, holding the full to-go cup between my hands.

I did, but I wanted to leave because sticking around made me feel desperate. That I was lingering because I wanted some scraps of praise from him, that I really did want to be beautiful. Except after what I did to him, sticking around only made me feel like I was desperate for exactly that: attention and affection from a handsome man.

Besides, we learned last night the owner of the company, my boss's boss, was coming to town to inspect the progress of the resort and to go through the issues we were having. Jason, who didn't know his ass from his elbow because he consistently looked at mine–ass, not elbow, but I wouldn't be surprised if he eyed that too–expected a report to share, which meant I had papers to review. Numbers to crunch.

This guy was only being kind. Nothing more. It wasn't as if he'd be interested in me, regardless of the compliments he gave. Thinking there could be anything real was stupid, and everyone knew I wasn't that.

I wasn't looking for a man. In fact, after what happened at college and with Jason, all I wanted to do was hide. I definitely wasn't on a manhunt like my sister. Lindy wanted a husband and a family, and she wanted them five years ago. Of course, she was thirteen years older and as she said, her clock was ticking.

Me?

I wasn't even remotely close to getting my own shit together, let alone be girlfriend material. If Lindy saw me right now, she'd lose her shit that I was sitting here in public and hadn't done anything with my hair this morning besides pull it back in a hair tie. Or that I hadn't touched any of the makeup she'd given me as a passive aggressive Christmas present last year. Or any of the other reasons she'd find flaws with my appearance.

In front of this guy! God, I was being ridiculous,

drooling over him. Feeling things from his words when I shouldn't.

Beautiful.

Baby.

It was definitely time to go and get back to reality.

"Thanks for the cool shirt," he replied, pointing at his chest, but all I took notice of was how it highlighted every muscular inch of a man I couldn't have.

Even though he did everything he could to downplay what happened, I was embarrassed. So I tucked the pencil back behind my ear, pushed my glasses up and fled. Which I was as good at doing as math.

4

MAVERICK

FRIDAY 11:35 am

I COULDN'T GET the woman out of my head.

Bridge. The quietly beautiful, ridiculously smart, nerdy little thing from the coffee shop. Who'd spilled cold fucking coffee all over me and tried to dry me off with a handful of napkins. She was skittish and wary, sassy and shy. And fucking young. She also eyed me behind those thick glasses like I was a piece of candy and she wanted to get a lick.

Then she'd run out. Bolted like a horse out of the gate at the Kentucky Derby.

She wasn't like any woman I knew, and I'd been all over the world. Why did a tiny thing like her, who kept a pencil tucked behind her ear, distract me?

Like now, talking to Silas.

"Did you hear me?" he asked.

I blinked, getting visions of freckles and green eyes out of my head and on my brother's scruffy face. "No, what?"

"I asked you what the hell are you wearing."

I had him on video chat as I leaned against my car. I was at the site, getting my first glimpse of the resort since ground breaking two months earlier. His face, so similar to mine, filled my cell's screen. There were four of us James brothers–with me being the oldest–but only Silas ran the family business with me. Theo and Dex never had any interest. Theo decided to save the world by being a doctor and Dex got all the athletic genes and played pro hockey.

I frowned, glanced down, then grinned.

"Coffee shop t-shirt," I told him, remembering how I got it. How Bridge's little hands patting me down was the closest contact I've had to a woman in far too long.

"It's pink."

"Sure is."

"Going local already? You've been there... three hours."

"Someone ran into me with a cup of coffee."

A wince crossed his face. "You look way too happy for having your nipples burned off."

I rolled my eyes. "Iced coffee, thankfully."

"So what gives then?"

"A pretty woman did it." My mind drifted to those full lips and wide hips.

He laughed. "What about Farrah?"

My smile dropped. "What about her?"

"Word on the street is you're together."

"You know we're not. At all."

Farrah and I had grown up together and our parents had playfully suggested we should marry. That never went away. These days, we ran interference for each other, being each other's date as needed to social events.

I only had sisterly affection for her, and she didn't want me in return.

The fact that Silas brought her up was another reminder as to the gossip mill of the rich and famous. Being in Montana would hopefully avoid that.

"Mom wants grandchildren and as oldest–"

"She's not getting them from me and Farrah," I countered. I had the baby convo with my mother on a consistent basis. She had four single sons with no grandchildren on the horizon.

"Fine, fine. You were almost drowned by a cup of iced coffee and a pretty woman. Have a fling. When was the last time you were laid?"

I frowned, not sure if I should feel good he thought I could pick up a woman at a coffee shop and then fuck her, or depressed that he pointed out I hadn't gotten any in a long ass time.

"I'm not that much of a player." I wasn't. I didn't want to think how long it'd been since I had a woman in my bed. Not that I wasn't up for a little fun, but a quickie just didn't do it for me any longer. Nameless hookups had been fine in my twenties. I wasn't that shallow, but some women were, especially when they learned my last name and the number of zeros in my bank account. They wanted to fuck their way into a billion-dollar marriage so I always kept it casual.

"And it hasn't been that long," I added on a grumble.

He only laughed because he knew I lied.

"Besides, she's young." I followed that with a frown, thinking of how incompatible Bridge and I were.

"So? Is she legal?"

I didn't know for sure, but based on the conversation I overheard, she had a job that involved math, not a trig test in high school.

"Yes."

"Then what's the issue?"

I didn't answer right away, and he caught on.

"You think because your dick gets hard for a younger woman that you're like Dad?"

"He didn't fuck anyone over the age of twenty-five."

After my mom finally divorced him for having an affair with yet another secretary or caddy girl, he kept right on going with the young ones. Even having died of a heart attack while fucking one of them.

"Well, you have. And you're nothing like him," he told me. "You're thirty-seven years old. Go fuck who you want. Move away from home. Seriously. Stay there. Have babies with a twenty-something hottie. Make Mom happy."

"Babies? She spilled coffee on me and I'm attracted. I'm not planning on inseminating her." *Jesus.*

"Fine. Leave the semen out of it. Wear a condom. But go for it."

Go for it. The idea of peeling Bridge's clothes off and seeing all her secrets beneath was what I wanted to do now. I imagined–and with pretty dirty fucking thoughts–she would be lush and soft and perfect. I wondered how far her blush spread beneath her shirt.

I also wondered what she'd look like with my cum splashed all over her.

"I think I scared her off," I admitted.

I wasn't sure how I did that–since I hadn't said any of my dirty thoughts aloud–doing everything I could to reassure her I wasn't mad about the spill. I even held her hand and called her baby. I'd never done that before, called anyone baby, but it just seemed... right.

"You are a big, scary motherfucker."

Was that it? Was it because at first glance, I really was a big, scary motherfucker? I'd tried to be gentle, to protect her. Even from me.

"You're an inch taller," I countered. The James men all ate their vegetables as kids.

"It's a small town. Maybe you'll run into her. Your wardrobe hopes not literally. Pink definitely isn't your color."

I'd sacrifice another shirt to see her again.

"What's the status with the project?" he asked, steering away from my encounter earlier and onto why I was in Montana in the first place.

"Definitely behind." Turning my cell away from me, I offer him a slow scan of the site before facing him again. A crew was busy building out the second story, a few men pushing up a section of wall and anchoring it in place. The hum of an air compressor followed by the thwap, thwap of a nail gun filled the air.

The resort would have fifteen rooms. A five-star restaurant. Spa. Outdoor adventure center. Now? It didn't even have a roof.

"It'll get done."

"Before you retire?" he poked.

We were close, too fucking close sometimes, especially since we worked side by side. I may be CEO, but he ran James Corp just as much as me. We were close with Theo and Dex, too, up in each other's business non-stop and I was surprised one or both weren't also on this call.

"Fuck you. I'm not that old." Thirty-seven wasn't ancient, except when I seemed to have the hots for someone at least a decade younger. Maybe Bridge thought I *was* old. My dick didn't care. I'd had a semi since she patted me down and thinking of her naked with just a pencil behind her ear had me shifting my dick in my jeans.

"The project's that behind," he clarified.

I sighed because he was right. "I have a meeting in a few with the contractor." I flicked my gaze to the resort, currently it was nothing more than framed out.

"I'll come up."

I shook my head. "To do what? Kick someone's ass for me?"

"You are scrawny."

No response was needed for that because I hadn't been scrawny since the second grade.

"Let me see what the hell's going on. Unless you can build trusses or operate a crane, you aren't going to be of much help."

That was the next step. Once the second-floor framing was done, trusses would be lowered to build out the roofline. Then it could be enclosed and the roof put on. Hopefully before the snow started. Here in Montana, that came sooner than later.

"You can't do that shit either."

I smirked. "No, but I can hopefully scare the project manager into getting his shit together. I'll be back in the office by lunchtime tomorrow."

"You're not that scary in pink. But go bust some balls, brother."

I'd do it, because I wasn't having this project fail. I could throw more money at it, and I would, but that wasn't my way. The project team was failing at their job, and I needed to find out why.

5

BRIDGET

Friday 12:18 pm - Six hours before the scream

I ENTERED THE OFFICE, loaded down with bags from the deli. The meeting with Maverick James from Denver had started ten minutes ago, but my job wasn't to sit in on it, but to feed everyone.

After the coffee shop fiasco, I'd settled in at my desk and finalized the reports for my boss. He'd taken the printout I handed him, tore off the top sheet with my name on it, tossed it into the recycle bin, then told me to get everyone's lunch order.

Jemma, the office receptionist, had given me a
commiserating look and helped. She couldn't leave
her desk since she had to answer phones. I, on the
other hand, had free time to run out since I hadn't
been invited to the meeting.

She was well aware of how much of a little shit
Jason was, but neither of us had any way to complain.
There was no human resources locally, only at James
Corp headquarters in Denver. Since he'd come from
that office, it didn't seem like they were interested in
him being an asshole. He was a misogynist who liked
me as an assistant so he could ogle my ass and use my
brain to his advantage.

Jemma and I were the only locals hired to James
Corp for the project, the rest came from Denver with
Jason to be the core crew. A local general contractor
dealt with the various elements of the work such as
sub-contracting for concrete and electrical.

I didn't want to lose my job, but Jemma was a
single mother who needed the steady paycheck and
didn't dare complain. While I didn't have kids, I was
saving up money so I didn't have to live with my sister
for much longer.

So when I pushed through the front entry, barely
able to see over the tops of the bags, Jemma dashed

around her desk and opened the conference room door for me.

"The shingles are behind at the manufacturers in Salt Lake. Delivery delays."

I didn't look up as I set the bags down on the large table as Jason spoke, pulling out wrapped sandwiches and reading the scrawl on them to figure out what kind they were.

It was the lack of response that had me lifting my gaze.

Everyone was staring at me. Jason. Ed, the engineer. Bixby, the local general contractor. And–

Him.

The guy from the coffee shop. He was the only person in the room I didn't know, which meant he was–

Holy crap.

Maverick James.

I spilled coffee all over my boss's boss. One of the James Corporation's owners.

I made a billionaire boss wear a pink Steaming Hotties t-shirt.

I stared at him. He stared at me. I tried not to cower because... God. His eyes narrowed.

"Bridget's brought lunch. Your assistant shared that you liked roast beef."

Jason's words had me blinking and I'd never been so thankful for the task of playing waitress, pulling out and dispersing the sandwiches, bags of chips and cans of soda.

"Bridget?" His deep voice had me swallowing. Now I couldn't look his way if my life depended on it.

"Yes, my assistant," Jason prompted.

Ed and Bixby offered thanks as I handed them their food. We'd worked together earlier on the issues and I finalized them into the report. I liked them both, unlike Jason the Jerk.

I went around the table, set the roast beef before Maverick James. He stood and I had to tilt my head back to meet his gaze. I pushed my glasses up.

"Bridget Beckett." I reached my hand out to introduce myself, not because I hadn't done so at the coffee shop, which I hadn't, but because I was at work and it was the appropriate thing to do.

His big hand engulfed mine once again.

"Maverick James," he said, offering me a smile.

He stared.

I stared.

He stared some more.

I noticed his eyes were so brown as to be almost black. That whiskers had come in across his strong jaw since I saw him last. Two hours earlier. That someone was clearing their throat.

It wasn't me.

It wasn't Mr. James.

It was Jason. Shit... I yanked my hand back and spun on my heel. Heat filled my cheeks and I bolted out the door and leaned against the wall just outside the conference room as if my body weight was needed to hold it up.

Jemma swiveled her chair around behind her desk and grinned. "He's gorgeous, right?" she whispered so only I could hear and fanned herself, just like Eve had.

"What about the cost increases?" I heard Mr. James' voice through the open doorway.

"I've been working on a report for you," Jason replied.

I looked up at the ceiling tiles thinking of the report *I'd* worked on.

"Can I see it?" Mr. James asked. "I own the company and came personally from corporate, Jason, because the cost is up twenty-two percent and–"

"My assistant has it," he said, cutting him off and trying to quickly placate. "She fetches reports as well as she does food. Bridget!"

Asshole.

His shout had me pushing off the wall, then taking

a deep breath. I could do this. I could swallow down Jason's patronizing and misogyny while being in a room with Mr. James, who'd held my hand and called me beautiful. I grabbed a copy of the report from my desk and carried it in.

"I need the report," Jason said, although I had no idea why he hadn't brought in the one I gave him earlier.

I held the stapled pages up letting him know I had them, then handed them to Mr. James.

Mr. James' eyes met mine.

"Thank you," he said, his voice much softer than what he'd used for Jason's scolding. I was halfway to the door when he called out. "Take a seat, Bridget."

I glanced his way, then at Ed and Bixby, who only shrugged. They were both easy going and helpful, and also not big fans of Jason. Since he ran the project, they did what he said, even if it had been messing with the entire project. Enough that the CEO himself was here.

I pulled out a chair and settled into it at the far end of the huge table from Mr. James.

Mr. James unwrapped his sandwich and Ed and Bixby followed after. I sat with my hands folded in my lap.

"Aren't you eating, Bridget?" Mr. James asked when

he noticed I was the only one without a lunch.

I pushed my glasses up again. "I'll... I'll eat later, Mr. James."

"Maverick," he corrected. "And your answer means you didn't get a sandwich for yourself." He picked up one half of his sub and stood, carrying it along with a few napkins, around the table and set it in front of me. "Eat."

I looked from him to the others, then looked down, not wanting to draw attention to myself. The last thing I expected was to be part of this meeting.

Mr. James–Maverick–settled in his seat, waited for me to take a bite of the sandwich before he took one of his own. As he chewed, he opened the report and scanned it.

"Tell me about this," he said to Jason.

"Bixby," Jason said, diverting. He shoved a huge bite of ham and cheese into his mouth most likely so he wouldn't have to answer anything else.

Bixby was in his late thirties, a few years older than my sister. He grew up here in the valley like I had, but we were far enough apart in age that we didn't cross paths much. He'd been running his family's construction company with his father since college, but his dad had retired a few years ago and he ran it solo now. He loved to ski and played the banjo of all things.

"There was some confusion with the size of the event space," Bixby explained. "The square footage was off. That was the basis for the cost variation."

The event space was for weddings and other celebrations and connected to the inn by an enclosed breezeway.

"Two thousand, five hundred sixty-six and a half square feet instead of two thousand eight hundred something," Maverick said, making my head whip up.

Maverick wasn't looking at the report, he was looking at Bixby as he shared the numbers.

A piece of shredded lettuce fell from my mouth, and I grabbed a napkin to conceal my chewing. And amazement. Because those were the numbers I'd told Bixby on the phone at the coffee shop. Maverick had heard my half of the conversation and remembered them.

Bixby's eyes widened, then he grinned. "That's right. You'll find the costs will be more in line with the original projections with that fix. Schedule, too."

Maverick nodded. "Good. That's good news, Jason."

I set my sandwich down, watched as Jason preened under Maverick's praise. For work he didn't do. Suddenly, I wasn't hungry. Or happy.

6

MAVERICK

JASON JIMENEZ WAS A DICK. I didn't like him the second he gave me a limp handshake and I still didn't like him now. I knew his type. Middle management that coasted for decades on doing as little work as possible. It was clear he considered Bridget–a name a hell of a lot better than Bridge–nothing more than a servant instead of an assistant made me wonder how he hadn't gotten fired before now. It was obvious he'd been hired during my father's tenure as CEO and hidden himself, and his behavior, well since I took over.

Not any longer.

It was the way he looked at Bridget's ass that had

me furious. Knowing Bridget from the few minutes at the coffee shop, she wouldn't speak up about his behavior. Wouldn't knee him in the balls and tell him to fuck off.

I wanted to do it, to tell him to fuck off, but not yet. I was thankful I'd overheard Bridget's conversation earlier. It was clear now that it was with Bixby, the local contractor, she'd been talking to. He seemed a decent sort, knowing his stuff and admitting when there was a mistake. He wasn't planning on billing tens of thousands of dollars for a math error.

As I listened to Ed, the engineer, and Bixby, give updates on everything from wiring codes to truss delivery, I didn't miss a thing Bridget did. Which was nothing.

When she'd first come in with the food, I'd been stunned. Amazed that fate had made it easy for me to see her again. When she'd finally looked my way, she'd been just as surprised.

She had no idea who I was when she'd run into me, that was clear.

I'd thought she was beautiful before, and I'd told her that. But now?

Fuck, she was... lovely. I'd been right to be distracted. With her hair pulled back, her high cheekbones were prominent. Those green eyes were even more brilliant behind her glasses than earlier. She wore not a lick of makeup which only high-lighted how naturally beautiful she was. A spray of freckles across her upturned nose wasn't hidden by thick foundation. Her lips were the prettiest shade of pink and not from a tube of color. They were full. Kissable.

I'd tried to get her to eat, because no way in hell was she serving us and then not having any herself, but she'd stopped the second I gave Jimenez a little credit.

The petty fucker hadn't shared who really earned the praise when I tested him. He took it and kept it for himself.

Because of that, Bridget had shut down. Her gaze never left the sandwich in front of her as her shoulders slumped. As if she hid herself away behind her glasses and plain clothes. Her brightness was gone.

When Ed and Bixby finished their sandwiches, they ducked out to get back to work. I'd agreed to stop by the job site later so they could walk me through it. They seemed happier with that than stuck here with Jason.

Bridget left the room with them, trying not to be noticed, but that was impossible.

I caught Jimenez's eyes on her retreating form.

I cleared my throat and gripped the edge of the table.

He turned back, a smirk on his face. He leaned in, lowered his voice. "That young ass is a piece of work. So are her tits. I'm not sure if I like her better coming or going."

From outside the opened door, I heard a little gasp.

I stood, pissed. I didn't like Jimenez's locker room talk, clearly done to seem like we were buddies. Two guys sitting around while the little woman served them and then moved on to ogle and demean her. Jesus, he reminded me of my father's behavior. Women had to be pretty, willing to fuck, and dumb. Interchangeable.

This was not fucking happening. Especially when Jimenez didn't give a shit that Bridget overheard what he'd just said about her. Not with me as CEO of James Corp. Not with any woman and especially not with Bridget.

His words, I completely agreed with, which made me feel like an asshole. An old asshole lusting after someone so young. I wasn't sure if I liked her ass or tits better either, but that wasn't something I was going to share. With anyone. I wanted to get my hands on her, but to make her feel good, to make her feel beautiful. Special. Not degraded.

"Tell me, Jason, how did you discover the square footage discrepancy?" I asked, trying not to grit my teeth, or put my fist through his.

He hopped to his feet, the wheeled chair rolling back. "Well, I... the math didn't add up."

"Right, but you shared a cost increase last week. Didn't you think that was a big jump?"

"Yes, I–" he sputtered, but I cut him off. I didn't need to have him spew any more of his bullshit.

"It was enough that I flew up here to meet with you."

"The report shows the fix," he countered.

"Because your assistant found it, isn't that right?"

I might have been in a pink t-shirt, but I was still the boss. And pissed. I crossed my arms over my chest and Jimenez swallowed hard.

"It's her job to assist me when issues like these arise."

"Like doing the math." I grabbed the report and tossed it so it slid across the table to stop in front of him. "Show me where the fix is."

He picked up the papers, leafed through them. His face flushed as he fumbled. I waited.

"Just give me a moment," he said.

"You can't show me because you have no clue."

He dropped the papers and rolled his shoulders

back. "My assistant pulled the document together. Bridget!"

She slinked into the doorway but entered no further.

"Show Mr. James where the fix is in the report."

With a hand raised, I stopped her. "No need. It's clear who's done the work on this project."

Bridget looked up and her eyes widened. Her surprise made me realize her upset over lunch wasn't because of Jimenez, but because of me. I'd backed the fucker when I'd tested him, only she didn't know it was a test.

Shit. Knowing I'd made her weak was like a kick to the gut. The last thing I wanted was for her to hate me, or worse, lump me in with a fucker like Jason Jimenez.

That wasn't going to happen because I wanted to see her smile. I wanted to be the one to make her do it. And so many other things. Jimenez was going to be on the next flight out of the valley and off my payroll. And as far away from Bridget as possible.

I stepped toward him, and he retreated. "It's also clear that you haven't taken the sexual harassment class that's required annually for all employees," I pushed, referring to the one I'd put in place the first week I took over the company after my father died, "because if you did, you'd know there's a zero-tolerance policy for comments like yours. That shit doesn't fly with me."

I stepped around him, stopped in front of Bridget and winked. The only person who was going to think dirty thoughts about her was me. At the same time, I wanted to pull her into my arms, hug her and tell her she was safe from assholes, but she didn't need a man touching her right now. Not me, at least not until I made things right.

"Excuse me, Jemma?" I called.

She stood from her desk and faced me. I could clearly see hope in her eyes. Yeah, she'd been fucked over by Jimenez too. I was sure of it.

"Can you please book Jason a flight today back to Denver?"

Her mouth dropped open, but she snapped it shut, then smiled. "My pleasure, Mr. James."

I had no doubt that was true.

"Are you fucking kidding me?" Jimenez shouted. "You're firing me because these women can't handle a little talk?" His arms flailed as he spoke, then wiped spit from his mouth with the back of his hand.

"I'm firing you because not only do you not do your job, you're a little shit who has to demean women to make his dick seem big," I said. It was really fucking hard not to toss him out, but I was the boss, and this was a James Corp office, no matter how small.

Jimenez pulled his arm back with a blatant haymaker I could see coming, and let it fly. I could have blocked it, but I didn't. It glanced off my jaw and barely rocked my head back.

Bridget hadn't moved from the doorway, but her hand was over her mouth watching the confrontation.

"You saw that, right?" I asked her, making sure it was clear who threw the first punch.

She nodded, her eyes wide behind her glasses.

Not eager to fight in front of her–because this side of me was the last version I wanted her to see–but I had no choice. I wouldn't let this go. I couldn't and I wanted her to know it. I fucking needed her to know I would protect her.

I gave Jimenez one quick jab in return. His head rocked back, and he fell to his ass. Secretly, the sound of his nose breaking gave me immense satisfaction.

Immediately, I turned to Bridget.

"Are you okay?" I asked. She seemed fine, but I had no idea how long this had been going on for or what he'd said or done in the past. Had it just been words, or had he touched her?

She nodded.

"Can you call the sheriff for me, ba–Bridget?" I

wanted to call her baby, but after the way I had just outlined the sexual harassment rules of the company, I didn't want to break them myself.

Bridget nodded and went to her desk.

"I won't press charges if they can escort him to the plane and ensure he gets on it," I added, keeping my eyes on Jimenez. He wasn't getting up, which was the smartest thing he probably did all day.

I settled my hands on my hips and took a breath. Fuck. I was supposed to be in and out of Hunter Valley. Not only was the project behind, but now there was no project manager.

It looked like I was staying in town for a while and surprisingly, I wasn't bothered by the idea. In fact, it was Bridget, on the phone with the sheriff, who had me looking forward to staying.

7

BRIDGET

Friday 6:18 pm

I SCREAMED.

In the middle of Kincaids, the bar's outdoor patio loaded with people.

Not because I saw a mouse or a spider, but I just realized I'd sent a sex quiz to the guy who signed my paychecks, the same guy who I'd been lusting after for the past eight hours. It was more frightening than the scariest horror film ever made.

Worse than leaving MIT ashamed and broken. Worse than... anything that had ever happened to me, and there had been a lot.

Everyone on the deck stopped talking and stared, and I couldn't be any more embarrassed if I tried. I stared at my email's Sent folder, the recipient's name crystal clear.

Maverick James.

Not Mallory Mornay.

The little paperclip and *Sex Quiz* file name confirmed the worst.

I looked up at Mallory, freaking out.

"Oh my God."

Mallory snagged my phone while I wondered if it was possible to actually die from mortification.

"I just sent a sex quiz to Maverick James."

"Is everything okay?" Payton asked when she came over.

The other women clustered around me and Mallory in a full circle, blocking out the entire bar. "Did you see a rat or something?" Nora wondered, glancing down at the floor.

I pleaded with my eyes to Mallory not to tell them what happened. I couldn't bear it if all of them knew.

Being best friends since forever, she winked, then

offered the group an eye roll and a toss of her blonde hair. "A sale on her favorite calculator ended yesterday," Mallory said, waving a hand in the air. "You know how Bridge is about her electronics."

If I was thinking clearly, I'd take time wondering why they bought into that lie so easily and went back to the high-top table where they'd been settled.

I hadn't seen Maverick for hours. Not since he'd walked beside Hunter, the sheriff–yes, he'd been named after the town–as he escorted Jason to the patrol car. Maverick had gotten into his own car and followed out of the lot. I didn't know if he'd gone to the station or gone to the job site as planned. Or both.

What Maverick had done had been exhilarating. Not only had my douchey boss been fired and kicked out of the state, he'd been called out because he hadn't done any work *and* because he was a creep. I didn't usually like confrontation, but this one had made me... hot.

He'd been like a cowboy in a white hat in a gun fight or a knight saving a maiden from a dragon.

Or a really hot man taking care of his woman.

Not that I was his woman. I wasn't. Not at all.

But my panties had gotten wet from it. From the way Jemma fanned herself all afternoon, I was sure hers had too, but I didn't want to think about that. In fact, I didn't want any other woman thinking Maverick was hot.

Because I sure as hell did. There wasn't a thing about Maverick James that I didn't find attractive. None of it was diminished by him in a pink t-shirt either.

Was I any better than Jason, ogling and thinking naughty thoughts about a coworker? One who'd been nothing but kind to me? He'd read the email I'd mistakenly sent him and question my integrity. Perhaps even assume I was like Jason who sexually harassed people.

God, what if he thought I'd led Jason on? That his inappropriate words weren't one sided?

It could be like MIT all over again. My professor had seduced me into his bed so he could take my theoretical math research and use it in a professional paper of his own, only discovering this after I submitted my thesis for review and been accused of plagiarizing. That had been bad.

My stomach lurched and so much adrenaline was pumping through my bloodstream that my fingers tingled.

I grabbed Mallory's arm. "I have to get that email."

She winced and pried my fingers off. "Easy there," she said, looking over her shoulder and made a finger curling gesture to Payton, who came over with a shot glass filled to the brim with a clear liquid. Mallory passed it to me. "First off, drink that."

"Getting me drunk isn't going to help," I snapped.

Her pale brow winged up. "It's not going to hurt," she countered.

Conversation on the deck returned as if some crazy lady hadn't just made a scene.

"I'm going to lose my job," I told her, staring at the shot, then tossing it back. I coughed, then winced as it burned all the way down. "Worse, Mal, he's going to think I'm just like my professor."

She leaned in close so all I could see was her. "Your professor lied, got you into bed and took your research and used it as his own. How is that even the same?"

Hearing her give a shotty recap of why I left MIT didn't make me feel any better. "Maverick James will think Jason's sexual harassment wasn't one sided. I sent him a *sex* quiz. The title alone could get me fired. And if he reads it?"

I swallowed hard, willing the shot not to come back up.

"He'll find it funny. I do. Unless you put his name on the last question." Her eyes widened in panic. "Oh my God, please tell me you wrote you want to have sex with him."

She was too excited about my stupidity for me to admit that if there was any guy I would want to sleep with, it would be Maverick James. But I kept that to myself.

"No, I didn't put him."

She stilled. Frowned. "Wait. Then who did you put? Are you hot for a local I don't know about? I'm your best friend and you're supposed to–"

"I put Jake Ryan."

She blinked. Then laughed. "The hero from *Sixteen Candles.* You put in the exact same answer as Samantha Baker did in the movie."

"I know. You were rushing me and he's hot."

"He wears a sweater vest."

"He's still hot and you know it."

She sighed. "He is. But, God, Bridge… this would only happen to you."

I ignored the fact that she was humored by my fuckup. "He told Jason there's a zero tolerance policy for sexual harassment. Zero. I am going to lose my job," I repeated. "I *need* that job. I mean, I can't tell Lindy I dropped out of MIT so I can work for Eve at the coffee shop."

"Lindy needs to chill the fuck out," Mal countered.

My sister was wound tighter than anyone I knew and I'd never known her once, ever, chill the fuck out.

"Who cares if you lose that job? It's been shitty from the start. I mean, you can be a teacher. The Physics teacher at the high school is going on maternity leave. Teenagers have to be better than sleazy bosses. Besides, you're the only person I know who loves that shit. Physics and math, not sleazy bosses."

"While I agree with that, about Lindy chilling out, and the fact that I loved Physics class in high school, it doesn't solve my problem. Neither does the teaching job since it's summer break. I have to deal with the one I currently have, the one I *think* I currently have. The only way to do that is to delete that email."

"But you didn't name your boss as the guy you want to bang so you didn't specifically sexually harass him."

"Will you quiet down?" I breathed, glancing around.

"The music's too loud for anyone to hear us, and besides, everyone in here is talking about banging."

Probably true.

"You're freaking out more than usual." She held up her hand. "I'm not diminishing the issue with your professor, but not every guy is a dickwad like him. What's the deal with Maverick James? I saw that he's hot, and big, like break-your-vagina big."

I winced and gave her the full story. "I ran into him at the coffee shop this morning."

"So?"

I didn't stop wincing. "I mean *literally* ran into him. I drowned him in my iced coffee."

Mallory pinched her lips between her teeth to keep from laughing at me.

"Then he told me it was no big deal. Maverick held my hand and called me beautiful and baby and–"

"Maverick? Not Mr. James? Whoa. I think you should marry this guy."

"Don't write your maid of honor speech yet."

"I'm your maid of honor?" she asked, a sappy smile on her face.

"At my not-real wedding? Yes," I countered; my words laced with sarcasm. "Back to the point? I embarrassed myself this morning with the coffee and now this. I have to delete that email." If my eyes could glow red, she'd finally get how serious I was.

She thought for a moment. "Fine. We have to get that email. How?"

A guy walked by and Mal took a moment to eye him up and down. "Speaking of banging..."

I tapped her on the forehead, gave her a pointed look. "He left his laptop at the office when he left earlier. He hadn't come back for it when I came here.

It's probably still there. I'll go on it, find the email and delete it."

She tipped her head to the side and studied me.

"What?" I asked, wiping my mouth, thinking I dribbled the shot or something.

"Who are you and what happened to my best friend?"

I straightened my spine. "What? You think I'm Boring Bridget?"

She tucked her hair behind her ear. "No, you idiot. This is a reckless idea. You don't do reckless. You calculate the risks on everything. Remember the time you analyzed the data on losing bikini tops on that water slide at Splash Mountain?"

It was a smart review because my fifteen-year-old self did not want to flash the entire water park because of a dangerous combination of velocity, angle of slope and durability of spandex.

"I'd rather show my boobs to this bar than have Maverick James see the email."

Her mouth fell open because I was that serious. "What did you put in that sex quiz?"

I ignored her question. "I calculated the risk you're talking about. It's being fired. If I don't delete that email, I *will* be fired."

I remembered how serious Maverick was about

Jason's behavior. No chance he would let this slide with me. Or anyone.

"Okay, Brave Bridget," she said, oddly triumphantly, hooking my arm through hers. "Let's go get that email. Hopefully, he hasn't read it yet."

8

MAVERICK

I READ THE EMAIL. Well, the email itself was blank, but the attachment? Holy shit.

If the sender hadn't been listed as Bridget Beckett, I wouldn't have believed it came from her. Not after the other email she'd sent me with the updated cost breakdown and schedule which had been boring, mathematically accurate and thorough.

This? It was a fucking sex quiz.

Or a quiz on fucking.

After reading the answers–twice–it gave me a shit ton of insight into my latest obsession. And it made sense. And I'd never been so hard.

I read the first question.

On a scale of 1 to 10, how kinky you are?

I dropped into the office chair, then winced, because my dick pressed painfully against the zipper of my jeans. This wasn't porn, nothing remotely like that. But it was an insight into someone's mind, into their naughtiest thoughts.

And they were Bridget's.

I'd seen interest in her eyes when she wasn't blushing and looking away.

But this? Knowing the woman I wanted to get beneath me and scream my name had completed a sex quiz? I was in big fucking trouble.

Why would she send it to me?

She wouldn't. There was no text in the main email, only the attachment.

She'd sent it to me by mistake. It was the only answer. There was no way in hell she'd email me this. Which made me a dirty old man reading the responses of a woman who had to be twenty-one or twenty-two. I might have weighed over two hundred pounds, but I was only so strong. It was ridiculous how a woman so small, so... perfect, could bring me to my knees.

So I read it with the eagerness of a twelve-year-old with his first Playboy.

No comment.

Bridget hadn't given a rating for how kinky she was. Maybe she didn't know. That meant she needed to find out and I was going to be the one to show her. Would she like toys, blindfolds? Fuck, would she like to be tied to the headboard and have her pussy licked? What about exhibitionism? Hell, no. No one would see her body or what she looked like getting fucked besides me.

Shit. I was in trouble here and I was hard from a "no comment" response.

If you didn't answer, is it because you are a virgin?

Bridget had typed NO. In all caps. Meaning she slept with every guy in Hunter Valley or that she had her caps lock stuck on?

While my own kink of popping her cherry was making me shift in my chair, there was nothing wrong with her having had sex before. She wasn't *that* young.

How many partners have you had?

She typed in 1. One? Fuck, yes. One. Her no comment answer to the kink question made more sense. It wasn't like someone figured out their naughtiest kinks with their first sexual partner, unless that partner was really skilled... and kinky.

Now I needed to go on a manhunt and kill Mr. 1.

What's the one thing you wish you got from your partners?

Orgasms.

I groaned. Literally closed my eyes and groaned. Now I really wanted to track down Mr. 1 and beat the shit out of him for not being a gentleman. A lady always came first. Always.

Or I should thank him because the first time she came with a guy was going to be with me. On my fingers, my mouth, my dick. Any of them. ALL OF THEM.

I was suddenly very possessive of Bridget Beckett's orgasms.

I stood, adjusted my dick, then paced. Fuck, it was hot in here.

Leaning down, I set a hand on the desk beside my laptop, read the next quiz question.

What do you want a guy to do to you in bed? This is anonymous so share your darkest fantasy.

Yes, Bridget... what was your darkest fantasy?

To get on my knees.

I pushed up to standing. Blinked. Leaned back down. Read it again.

To get on my knees? To what, suck a guy's dick? To pray? To... I had no fucking idea, but the thought of her praying to my dick while it was touching the back of her throat had pre-cum dampening my boxers.

I had a problem. I wasn't any better than Jason. Probably a hell of a lot worse. Jason just wanted to make women feel like shit by seeing them only as sexual objects.

I... I wanted Bridget. In a sexual way. On her knees, like her fantasy. Hell, it was turning into my darkest fantasy as well.

But only with Bridget. In private. Where I gave her all the orgasms she'd never received.

It was completely different.

Who do you want to do it with? Name your dream lay.

"Who the fuck is Jake Ryan?" I snapped, my voice echoing off the empty office walls. I ran a hand through my hair, stared at the name.

Was that her boyfriend? A guy she was dating? A man in town she had the hots for?

"Fuck!" I shouted. I was lusting after a woman whose dream lay was some fucker named Jake Ryan. "Jesus, I'm totally messed up."

I closed the quiz, then slapped my laptop closed, went down the hall to the bathroom to splash some cold water on my face. Because a tiny little math nerd had brought me to *my* knees.

9

BRIDGET

"WHICH ONE IS HIS?" Mallory asked, following me into the empty office.

It was just as I'd left it not even thirty minutes earlier. It wasn't dark out, so the overhead lights weren't needed to see. I pointed to the far desk, the one no one ever used. When James Corp rented out this space in a small office building on the south edge of town, they'd overestimated on office size. Or someone got the math wrong.

"How are you going to get past his password?" she wondered.

"I hate you," I told her when she pointed out an

obvious roadblock in my plan. "I can go in the back way to the company's firewall and access the password system."

I dropped into the chair behind the desk.

"You can do that?" she asked, sidling up beside me. "You're like the computer geek on that TV show."

I didn't know which show she meant, and I wasn't going to ask. I really didn't want to know the comparison. It was probably some nerdy guy with a pocket protector.

I lifted the lid and the display illuminated.

"Huh." I pushed my glasses up and blinked. "It's not protected."

That shot I had back at the bar was long burned off. My heart was pumping so frantically that the liquor never had a chance to make me buzzed. But was I seeing this correctly? No password? There was only his home screen, which had a background photo of Maverick with three other guys. One looked a lot like him, but had a beard, so I assumed he was a brother. Were the other two brothers as well?

"Holy hot lineup," Mal murmured, leaning down for a closer look. "I'm not sure which one I'd pick."

I looked over my shoulder at her. "I didn't realize that was an option."

She rolled her eyes at me, then hip checked me in

the shoulder since it was at just the right height. "Come on. Have some fun."

"Your kind of fun got me in this situation in the first place," I reminded.

She wasn't to be distracted. "I won't pick Maverick because he's yours."

"He's not mine," I countered.

"He totally is. If you sent some random guy that sex quiz, you wouldn't be this freaked out."

"Yes, I would."

She turned and leaned against the edge of the desk so she faced me. "You're telling me if you sent the quiz to Bixby that you'd freak?"

"Bixby isn't random and would know you put me up to it."

"True. I'd pick him." She turned and pointed at the brother on the far right of the photo. With his light brown hair and wide grin, he was good looking. But nothing like Maverick.

God, I got hot just staring at him in a group photo. That wavy hair. That smile. Those eyes.

I clicked on his email icon and waited a second for his inbox to fill the screen.

"There!" Mallory shouted and pointed again.

A thrill shot through me. There was the email! I clicked on the little box beside it, a checkbox filling it when I did so, then slid my finger over the trackpad toward the delete button and–

"Looking for something?"

I hit Delete before I launched to my feet, knocking Mallory back a few steps, bumping into the water cooler and making the half-full water jug wobble.

"Maverick. I was... I just–"

The corner of his mouth turned up, probably thinking Mallory and I were two of the Three Stooges the way we'd reacted. He was still in the pink t-shirt and jeans. Every time I saw him, he was even more handsome.

Maybe it was the lack of harsh fluorescent lighting. Or maybe it was just my ovaries telling me he was the one they wanted to give an egg to.

"Email," I blurted. "I was checking your email."

I couldn't lie to save my life.

"Oh? I received the updated report."

I slapped the laptop lid down. "Yes, good. I sent it and worried you didn't get it. Since you're leaving tomorrow and all."

He took a step closer. "That's the thing about emails. I can get them wherever I am."

"You're Maverick James," Mallory said with all her extroverted powers. The way she was eyeing him like a pile of Halloween candy after a few hours of hardcore trick or treating made me have feelings–like jealousy–I didn't want to think about.

Maverick's gaze lingered on mine another moment, then met Mallory's.

"I am, but I don't know who you are."

She shrugged, waved her hand. "Oh, I'm Bridge's best friend. She wouldn't be here without me."

I glanced down at the desk, only looking at him through my lashes. And glasses.

"Yes, I have a feeling you're right," he murmured. It was amazing how someone so big could temper his voice to be almost... gentle.

"Bridge is more exciting and alluring than her shoes let on," Mallory told him.

My head whipped up. "Mallory!"

She shrugged. "What? It's true. Those shoes are awful."

Maverick was full on smiling now.

"I like your shirt," she said, pushing on.

Maverick looked down at his sculpted chest. "Thanks."

"You've only been here, what, a day and you're getting involved in the community."

"How do you know I just got to town?"

"Bridge told me *all* about you."

"Mallory!" I yelled again. I was probably the new

world record holder for the most embarrassing day. "Can you just stop talking?"

"You meet incredible people at this coffee shop," he murmured, referring to Steaming Hotties.

Oh. My. God.

His gaze was still on me. I could feel it.

"About getting involved in the community, I meant that you're participating in the Parade of Pooches," she replied, pointing at his broad chest.

He frowned, tugged at the shirt as if he missed something in the Steaming Hotties script. "Parade of Pooches?"

"Tomorrow is Hunter Valley's summer parade," she explained. "The county animal welfare group pairs up with volunteers to walk in the parade with shelter dogs to get them seen and adopted." Mallory twirled her finger. "On the back. It says you're a participant."

He glanced over his shoulder as if he could read what it said, then back at Mallory. "A pet charity? Sure. Sounds like fun. What do I have to do?"

Mallory set her hands on her hips and did a weird lean. "Not sure, but I'd just show up at the shelter in the morning. The parade starts at ten, so before that." She turned to me, gave me a stupid thumbs up. "He's handsome *and* nice. Good job, Bridge."

I let my eyes bug out, telling her without words to shut up.

"Are we all set with that email?" Mallory asked, finally getting us on track to get out of here.

I nodded. "Yes, all set."

Definitely. As if. Absolutely not.

She sighed, grinned. "Great. So tell me, Maverick, those guys in your wallpaper photo."

He jammed his thumbs into the front pocket of his jeans, clearly not expecting her whiplash of topics. "My brothers?"

"Three brothers. Wow. You're all hot as fuck because–what's the line in that movie?–your father's a weatherman?"

A deep laugh ripped from him, and I was stunned, comparing him to the growly, pissed off version from earlier. "I'm not sure which movie you're talking about, but no, our father was definitely not a weatherman."

Another film reference? The whole movie thing was what got me in this trouble in the first place. I needed to limit Mallory's screen time like a parent would a toddler.

"Since you're taken by Bridge and all, tell me about the guy on the right," she pushed as I gasped at her boldness.

"Light brown hair?" Maverick asked.

She nodded. "Needs a trim. Dimple in the right cheek. And a shave, although I don't mind a guy with a little scruff. Green shirt with sunglasses tucked into the pocket."

"You sound like a detective."

"First grade teacher. I'm just observant about some things."

"Like my brother?"

"Mmm," she replied, her eyes glazing over at only the thought of the man.

"I'll be sure to tell Theo you asked after him."

"Theo," she repeated, as if testing his name on her tongue. "Yes, tell Theo *all* about me."

I didn't say a word through all of this. I'd been caught red-handed on my boss's computer. If Mallory wanted to try to pick up Maverick's brother, she could have at it.

"Well, we should get going," I prodded. "Ladies' night, remember?"

I'd never once been so eager to get back to a crowded bar than right now.

"If you're done, sure," Mallory said with a shrug as if what was happening wasn't a big deal, stepping around the desk.

I followed.

"Bridget," Maverick called.

I stilled, spun on my ugly shoe covered foot. "Yes?"

"Can I talk to you for a minute? About that email?"

Oh shit. My pulse kicked up a notch and my palms began to sweat. "Right. The email. Sure."

He stared at me. I stared at him, then the industrial carpet-covered floor. Then the water cooler, then back at him.

"Okay, then," Mallory said, cutting into the uncomfortable silence. "I'll wait outside."

She bolted before I could tell her not to leave me.

Maverick took a step closer, then another, until he loomed over me.

"The email," he said.

"Right." I licked my lips and his gaze dropped to my mouth. If he hadn't seen the sex quiz one, then he was talking about the project one I'd sent. "I'm happy to go over the schedule with you, or I can connect with your assistant to set up a meeting."

"I don't need Bradley to make dates for me."

I looked up at him, confused. "He makes dates for you all the–oh, you mean *dates.*"

"Yes. A date. You. Me."

I pushed my glasses up. "You're leaving tomorrow."

He shook his head. He wasn't the only brother who needed a haircut. While the sides were clipped fairly short, the top was long, and it swooped over his forehead.

"I'm not going back to Denver. I'm staying here. With Jimenez fired, I'll lead the project."

He wasn't leaving? "Oh."

He would be here for months.

"So, the email," he prodded. "I want to make those things happen. I want to do that with you."

I nodded. "Okay, well, I'm just the assistant and like I said, I can go over the schedule. The math again, but I feel confident it's accurate." I didn't want to add that, but he was now not only my boss's boss, but he was now my boss. God, that barely made any sense. The last thing I wanted to do was remind him of my freakish abilities with numbers because I'd be seeing him every day.

"I'm talking about the other email."

"The other–" My face flushed so hotly I was surprised the pink t-shirt didn't catch fire. "Oh God."

"Tell me, Bridget." He moved to stand in front of me, crossed his arms over his chest. "Who the hell is Jake Ryan?"

10

BRIDGET

WHO IS JAKE RYAN?

Oh my God, he was jealous of a movie character. I tried not to smile, biting my lower lip.

"Boyfriend?"

I shook my head.

"Fuck buddy?"

I was so stunned by the term that I huffed out a laugh. "What?"

"You heard me. I want to know what I'm up against here."

I stared at him, blinked. Blinked again. "You... you think you have competition?"

He shrugged. "You put his name down on an anonymous sex quiz as the guy you want to fuck."

"He's the guy in the movie *Sixteen Candles*. It's an eighties classic."

He stared at me like I was crazy. Eyes wide, mouth hanging a little open. Clearly, he needed more details.

"Samantha Baker fills out a sex quiz in study hall and instead of it getting to her best friend, Jake Ryan, her dream guy, picks it up and reads it. He becomes curious about her," I explained. There were so many side stories to the movie, I made sure to stay focused on the important parts. "This is because she put his name on it as the guy she wants to do it with. Plus, it's her sixteenth birthday and her family forgets. And... well, you know it?"

He scratched the back of his neck. "The movie?"

I nodded.

"No."

"Oh, well, then you should see it. It's good."

"Why are *you* completing a sex quiz?" he asked.

It was a really good question.

I sighed and glanced at the office door. "Mallory's a little crazy, if you didn't notice. We watched the movie recently and she got the ridiculous idea that all of her friends should complete a sex quiz and we'd share the answers at girls' night. Which is tonight."

"So you two took the movie plot more seriously than the others."

I frowned, then realized what he meant. "You mean me filling it out and it actually getting into the wrong person's hands? Definitely."

"Then I'm your Jake Ryan," he said simply.

I took a step back, held up my hand. There was no way I was admitting that. "Nope."

He advanced. "I am. You sent it to me. I read it. I'm curious about you, Samantha Baker."

"I'm not Samantha Baker and there's no way in hell you're Jake Ryan."

"Why not? Not cute enough?" he asked, mock offended.

I looked over his perfect, big body. "You're definitely not in high school. Besides, I don't think they make a sweater vest in your size."

"Sweater vest?" He looked down at himself, probably wondering where he could even buy one these days. "Can't be worse than a pink t-shirt."

He was probably right. He'd look good if he wore a potato sack. His hair was a little messier this late in the day and I wondered if that five o'clock shadow would be soft or raspy against my thighs.

Ugh!

Still, the guy who I was imagining eating me out

had seen the email before I deleted it. He knew the quiz was mine. He'd read it. Knew personal details about me, like my secret fantasy.

This was so, so bad.

"Look," I said, glancing at the ground and then up, up, up into his dark eyes. I'd made an epic mistake and it was going to cost me. But I wasn't going to deny or push blame or anything like Jason did. I owned my mistakes, to the point of dropping out of college. I didn't know what I was going to do, and I dreaded the inevitable explanation to my sister, but I'd been through worse. "I'm sorry. I apologize about the email. It was obviously not my intention to send it to you, but that doesn't matter in a situation like this."

"Situation like this?" he wondered. He scratched the side of his neck with a finger.

"I know your zero-tolerance policy on sexual harassment and I understand that I'm out of a job. I'll... I'll clean out my desk." I turned and made my way over to it because the sooner I was out of here, the better. I didn't have many personal effects, but I did have a lip balm and a few hair ties in the drawer.

"What?" he asked, following me to my desk. "You're not fired."

I looked up at him. His brow was creased, and he looked very, very confused.

"You own the company and I sent you an inappropriate email," I explained. I'd imagined Jason's actions earlier in the day were still fresh.

"By mistake," he added.

I shook my head. "It doesn't matter. I've offended you–"

"That's not what it did to me–"

"–and you shouldn't be subjected to that kind of–"

"–because if you'd just look at the front of my jeans you'd see that–"

"–what?" I snapped my mouth shut and my gaze dropped to his crotch. His jeans were well molded and I couldn't miss that he was hard. And big. The thick bulge of his dick curved down the inside of his thigh. I didn't even know they could do that. I stared, then blinked. Realized staring at him like this was worse probably than the email. "Sorry!"

I spun around, staring at the white board on the wall behind my desk.

"Bridget. Baby. Stop." He sighed, came over and turned me to face him. The heat of his gentle touch made my heart skip a beat.

His eyes shifted between mine and my mouth. Then back. "You're not fired. You can subject me to that kind of thing whenever you want. I'm not offended. I'm aroused."

Reaching out, he took my hand and placed it over his... holy shit.

I could feel the massive size of him, and I would swear it grew beneath my palm. I had to wonder if that thing would fit inside of me. The ridged edge of the crown was obvious and that would definitely be too big to handle. Right? My pussy clenched with an eagerness to give it a shot.

With his hand on top of mine, he pressed and I inadvertently squeezed. He groaned.

I made him hard. I made him groan. Me!

"See?"

He dropped my hand, then reached up, he tucked a strand of hair behind my ear. I was too stunned to retreat or respond.

"I'm going to kiss you now." His voice was deep and low as if telling me a secret.

Oh my God.

Slowly, he leaned in. He was waiting for me to tell him no and I couldn't say it. He brushed his lips with mine. I wanted him to kiss me. God, did I.

His lips were soft. Gentle. A caress.

Then he groaned.

Then they weren't. Gentle or a caress. His lips settled on mine. Claimed. Devoured. His big hand cupped the back of my neck, the other circling my waist and pulling me in tight. I felt every hard inch of him, including that super-sized cock pressing into my belly.

I moaned–because what woman wouldn't moan from a Maverick James kiss–and his tongue plunged. Found mine.

Holy shit. Now this was a kiss.

The world spun and I felt the wall at my back as he pressed me against it. Maverick's leg nestled between mine, then lifted so I was practically riding his hard thigh.

No, I was actually riding it. One big hand hooked behind my knee to lift my leg even further and I wrapped both of them around his waist. He was so large I couldn't cross my ankles. His hands cupped my butt and rolled me into him. Through our jeans, his dick rubbed just right over my clit.

I was wild and needy and craved the contact because if we kept this up, I might come. I felt small and protected. Desired. "God, you're big," I murmured. "I mean... not–"

"Compared to you, baby, fuck, you're tiny," he countered, kissing along my jaw to my ear. Then a spot behind it and holy crap, was this what it was supposed to feel like?

"Oh," I whispered, angling my head for him

because I was so turned on and we were only kissing. His scent swirled around me. Dark and I couldn't think enough to describe it.

"Baby. Fuck, you feel so good." His soft breath fanned my heated skin. "I'm going to be the man to make you come."

That was so hot and so... oh my God. It was just what I had been thinking, but him saying those words aloud made me remember.

"Wait. No. Wait. Stop."

Maverick lifted his head and he lowered me to my feet and stepped back. A tiny bit.

"What's the matter?" He wasn't touching me in any way, but I could feel the heat radiating from him. My nipples tingled from lack of contact.

"I... what you said." I licked my lips.

An aroused Maverick had a flush to his cheeks. A wildness to his gaze. Slick lips. Ragged breathing.

"What?" His dark eyes were fixed on my mouth.

"Why did you say you were the one to make me come?"

"Because no one has before, right?" He eyed me with clear determination, that this was a problem he wanted to solve. *Could* solve. I was a math whiz, but I had a feeling Maverick was a genius with a woman's body.

"What I wrote on the sex quiz," I whispered, clarifying that he knew secrets about me because of it. Ones I hadn't wanted to share. Suddenly, I felt ashamed all over again. I'd lost my head. Like in Boston. I was so smart that sometimes I saw things too closely, too clearly, that everything on the periphery was a blur. Like reasons why people did things. Professor Diego had used that weakness to get what he wanted. I'd thought he wanted me, not my work. Jason had also wanted my brain to do his work for him. He wanted to have sex with me, not because of me, but because I had the holes he liked to fuck. I meant nothing to him. I'd meant nothing to Professor Diego.

I'd vowed to learn from my mistakes, returning to Hunter Valley with my tail between my legs, ashamed. I'd hid, tried my best to not attract attention of assholes like Jason and what they wanted from me by wearing plain clothes. By hiding my femininity. It hadn't worked because I hadn't missed the things he told Maverick. That he liked my ass and tits, even beneath baggy clothes.

I didn't think Maverick was like Jason or Professor Diego, but I'd only met him this morning. Not even twelve hours earlier. And I'd spilled coffee all over him and because of me, he had to stay in Montana. If I'd been a guy, Jason wouldn't have behaved as he had and wouldn't have been fired. Maverick would be heading back to corporate and his regularly scheduled life.

It made no sense, his interest. Why would a guy like Maverick James, handsome billionaire, want me after all that had happened?

The answer was the sex quiz. I'd given him the inside knowledge on how to fuck me. A printed report.

"What?" he asked, running the back of his hand over his mouth. "You don't want to come? I'll make it so good."

I knew he would. So did my pussy, that clenched at his dirty words. "I'm not letting you fuck me because you mistakenly received the sex quiz."

Understanding dawned on his face. "Oh, baby. No."

I was embarrassed this morning. Stunned and a little scared of what happened with Jason earlier. This? Right now? I felt shame. Like I was easy because I was naïve.

"Why else, Maverick? I mean, look at me!" I moved to the side and he gave me room. I waved my arms in the air, then glanced down at my feet. "I'm wearing shit kickers. Mallory yelled at me earlier over them pretty much being cock blockers. I'm not wearing makeup and God, my clothes have no color or silky fabric or reveal a hint of cleavage. You can have any woman you want, so the only reason why you'd stoop to touch me is the quiz."

His eyes narrowed and I could tell he was mad. "I don't like how you're talking about yourself. I will take you over my knee if you keep that up, baby."

He and Mallory were in sync about how I should be punished, which pissed me off more.

"I'm not your baby!" I shouted.

"Wanna bet?"

I practically screeched and rubbed my hands over my face. God, this was like MIT all over again. I learned though, and even with that hot and heavy kissing, I wouldn't have sex with Maverick because of the email. Wouldn't feel trapped.

"I won't have sex with you because of that quiz. Is that why you aren't firing me? Using it as leverage?"

His eyes widened and it looked like I struck him speechless.

"Leverage? Fuck, baby. Let's get some things straight," he said eventually. His voice was soft. Calm, as if not to upset me further. "I want you. I've made that very obvious. My dick's hard enough to pound nails at the project site. I want you... *you,* not because of the quiz. If I've made you feel bad, that's on me. Not you. So don't for one second think that my lack of control means I think you're easy or cheap or come with a sex quiz manual. It's because you're hot as fuck and I want that date. A date between a man and a woman, not boss and employee."

I had no idea what to say to that, so I said nothing at all. This day couldn't possibly get any worse. My lips tingled from the kiss and my panties were ruined. My pussy throbbed and didn't understand why we stopped.

"You don't believe me."

I shook my head. I wanted to, but I'd been burned before. I couldn't flee my hometown like I did Boston to escape my stupid mistakes.

"That's for me to fix. I will, Bridget. I'll fix this. All of it."

11

MAVERICK

THE HOT WATER pounded my back as I stroked my dick from root to tip. I had to lean down because I was too tall for the shower head, bracing my forearm on the tile. My dick ached with the need to come, throbbing as I ran my thumb over the tip, smearing a drop of pre-cum.

I imagined it was Bridget gripping me, knowing her little fingers wouldn't fit all the way around. That she'd look up at me with those green eyes wondering if she was doing it right.

I'd cover her hand with mine, show her how I liked it.

A groan escaped as the base of my spine tingled. I was going to come. Fucking finally.

On the ride back to the hotel room my assistant reserved for me, my dick hadn't gotten the inner-office memo that Bridget was mad at me. That it wasn't getting inside her until I got some shit figured out. That my right hand was going to be tackling the job, just like it had for a while now. Only I had plenty of new images in my spank bank.

Even though she thought I was using a position of power to get in her panties, just like my father had often enough with a decade or two of secretaries, my dick hadn't gone down since Bridget rode my thigh back at the office.

I groaned again, remembering how she felt. Smelled. How she tasted. How she responded, even for such a short time. The sound of my strokes mixed with the hot spray.

I tightened my grip, stroked faster.

Then I remembered the way she moaned and whimpered. She'd been right there with me. The chemistry between us was off the charts. I couldn't remember a woman so responsive, although I couldn't remember any other woman.

My balls got tight and I rested my forehead against the tile. With a rough growl, I came in thick spurts.

Gritted my teeth. The release was so fucking powerful little black dots clouded my vision.

"Fuck," I said, trying to catch my breath.

I vowed to get her beneath me because it was going to be so good. Explosive. If I felt like this just thinking of her, having her might just kill me.

I shut off the water, sighed. Stepped out and grabbed a towel.

I was an asshole. I was an old man in comparison to her. Her boss. Hell, worse than that. I owned the fucking company. And I kissed her. In the office. No, that hadn't been kissing. If she hadn't stopped me, I'd have had her jeans dangling from one ankle and my dick so deep inside her she'd be squirming because it would be too much for her to take.

I had zero control with her. Why her? Why did she have to be so fucking young? I didn't understand how she made me this insane. Because that was the only explanation for how I was feeling.

She was clumsy and a touch awkward, which was endearing. She was also the victim of a–from what I could tell–a serial harasser for boss. Clearly, she hadn't felt able to defend herself or felt she had a resource for help. The fact that she thought I would use her sex quiz as *leverage* over her made me wonder if Jimenez was the only asshole in her life. If she'd dealt with other men like him, like my dad.

That last thought had me feeling ruthlessly protective of her. It wasn't because it was my responsibility as business owner to foster an environment of safety for all employees. She was young. A tiny thing. I wanted to hold her and listen to the list of men who fucked her over, then take that list and go beat the shit out of them. I wanted to do it because I knew the kind of man who did this shit and I refused to be like him.

I wanted to solve all her problems. Shoulder all her worries and fears because I was big enough to handle all of them.

Jason Jimenez, the fucker, was gone. I solved one of them.

And that quiz? It was, no doubt, meant to be silly and fun, like her friend Mallory. But for Bridget, it really was grounds for firing as she said. It also revealed her naughtiest thoughts which made my dick stir all over again.

She was exposed. Unprotected and with no safety net. How my father maintained his control. He made women vulnerable. Didn't give them a way out that offered them any kind of respect.

I had to give her one. I was the only person who

could ease her mind. Let her know she was safe with me. In her job, with her secrets and with her heart.

Yeah, that too. Because I was somehow falling for this woman. Age be damned.

The James Inn wasn't the only thing I had to work on here.

I realized just how to start fixing this mess as I left the steamy bathroom and traded the towel for boxers.

My cell pinged. I picked it up from the charger on the bedside table and read the text.

FARRAH - CALL ME.

I SIGHED. Not happening now. It was the second one from her today. She was my friend, but she'd have to wait. I had a different woman I had to tackle first.

Grabbing my laptop, I got to work.

12

BRIDGET

I REACHED into the dryer and pulled out a shirt, folded it and added it to the pile in my laundry basket. Lindy came in as I reached inside to grab the small pile of undies and socks that were left.

"Did you make a second pot of coffee?" she asked, leaning against the doorframe. She was in a pink nightie that skimmed her knees and matched her toenail polish. It had delicate lace edging around the neckline. Where I wore an old t-shirt to bed, Lindy wore actual bed things. Since she was a girlie-girl, that meant nighties. No sleep shorts. No pajamas. Short ones in summer, long ones in winter.

If there were two women any more opposite, it was me and my older sister. I had dark hair and green eyes like our father. She was blonde and blue eyed like our mother. I was small everywhere, she was tall and curvy. She was a perfectionist. I was… not. Even on a Saturday morning and having just rolled out of bed, she looked perfect. Her hair wasn't even messed up from her pillow because it was long and sleek and yeah, perfect.

She was always perfect. Because I was considered ridiculously smart, everyone imagined me to be perfect, too. Except that was such a bunch of shit. I was always a mess. The day before was a realistic indicator of how my life went.

I was in my running shorts and tank top, my sports bra straps showing. On my feet were my older sneakers, worn out from pounding the pavement around Hunter Valley. My hair was in a sloppy ponytail and my skin was sticky with dried sweat.

I'd already had my morning iced coffee, run six miles and started a second pot all before Lindy woke up. It wasn't that she slept late, but that I hadn't.

After being caught by my boss snooping on his laptop, then making out with him, I drove Mallory back to the bar, but I hadn't gotten out of the car. I'd driven straight home, afraid of anything else happening. She hadn't complained, probably because she knew I couldn't handle anything else about the printed sex quizzes.

I'd gone home and gone to bed, although I hadn't been able to sleep. I tossed and turned, thinking about the kiss. No, that had been full-on making out, the adult version. There was no fumbling like teenagers. That had been hot and... fuck. Insane.

After that, I shifted my thoughts to how Maverick had only wanted to kiss me–and press me against the wall and let me ride his thigh–because the sex quiz had given him permission to break out of the confines of what was office appropriate.

I'd called him on it, but he denied that was the reason for his actions. Or at least his half. I had zero reasons for mine other than I was obscenely attracted to him, and I'd been momentarily crazy.

Then he'd said he'd fix it.

I had no idea how he'd do that because the email had been sent. He'd read it.

Thoughts of how he'd accomplish that lingered until dawn, so I climbed from bed and decided to burn off my frustration and anger on a run. It hadn't helped. I wasn't sure what would. He'd said I wasn't fired. But what would it be like working with him every day after that kiss? With him knowing no man had given me orgasms? What my secret fantasy was.

How could I work with a man–Maverick, especially–who thought my secret fantasy was to suck his dick? Where was my credibility, my integrity, when all he would probably think of was me on my knees? He would never see me as a professional. I'd be demeaned and diminished like I had with my professor. Like Jason, even though he'd never touched me.

What I wrote was, in one context, exactly what I didn't want. A hard no. A safeword kind of limit. It was why I pushed Maverick away the night before.

"Earth to Bridge," Lindy said, waving her hand in the air.

I realized I'd thought all of that after she asked me after the coffee, socks dangling from my fingers.

"Sorry. Yes. I didn't sleep well."

"Things going okay at work?" The question held concern, but also had the tinge of motherly worry. While Lindy was my sister, she'd been my parent since I was ten when our parents died.

I frowned, tossing the socks into the basket. Tried not to panic that the sex quiz fiasco got back to her. "Why, what did you hear?"

She pushed off the wall and walked into the kitchen. The laundry was in a little hallway between it and the garage. "Nothing. I just assumed that's why you couldn't sleep. You're putting in a lot of hours."

"You said I could stay here as long as I had a job." This was a reminder of her tough love approach when I returned from Boston in the winter.

She sighed. "I didn't mean it like that."

"Yes, you did," I countered.

"No," she countered quickly, us falling into our usual pattern of her being disappointed in me and me defending myself. "You dropped out of school. Walked away from a full ride to MIT six months before graduation. It's school or real life and you made your choice."

Ouch. Again. I hadn't told her about what happened. About my professor. I told Mallory, but I knew she'd keep my secret. When I left Boston, my plan was to leave the anger, the heartache, all of it behind. It hadn't worked as I hoped, but I was getting better. Knowing I wasn't getting credit for all that work would piss me off forever. That a man was not only being lauded for it but gotten one over on me.

The fucker.

So, no. I hadn't told Lindy. Pseudo-mom. She was a perfectionist. Always striving. Always pushing. A control freak. Everything had to be just so, including me. Except I'd never be just as she wanted, no matter what I did. Whether I was a kid she was raising or a grownup, it didn't matter, so me leaving MIT only made me look like the wayward dropout that I officially was.

"Gotcha," I said, swallowing my pride. "I'll find an apartment soon."

She came over and hugged me. "That's not what I mean. God, I need more coffee. This is your house, too."

It was the house our parents bought when they got married. When they died, it went to Lindy. And since I'd been ten when the accident happened, I went to her, too.

"As for why I couldn't sleep, I was out with Mallory," I said, diverting her away from our usual argument of my off-track life. I grabbed the basket and set it on the kitchen table. "Ladies' night, remember?"

Lindy had been invited, like usual, but never joined us, telling me she felt too old to go out with my friends. She was thirteen years older and more mother than sister to me, so she had a point. It was probably weird for her to drink with me and Mallory since she had been the one who took us to ski lessons and bra shopping.

Now, I was thrilled that she hadn't joined us the night before. I didn't want to know her answers to the sex quiz, and I definitely didn't want her to know what happened with mine.

She returned to her coffee, grabbing milk from the fridge to top it off. She liked her coffee pale.

"Right." She took a sip, closed her eyes and sighed. "Maybe I should have gone with you. The guy last night was a disaster."

"That bad?" I asked, remembering she had a first date.

"His picture was from at least five years ago," she grumbled. "I don't care if a guy's losing his hair as long as he embraces it. Shave it all off. It's hot."

"No embracing?" I asked, trying to imagine this guy she'd swiped right on in a dating app.

"Comb over. Or more like Homer Simpson's three strands of hair. There was no embracing. Of me either."

I crossed the kitchen, set my hand on her forearm. She smelled like Lily of the Valley, her favorite scent. "Sorry. There's a guy out there for you."

"I'm thirty-five and I know every guy in Hunter Valley. They're either too old, too young or too wrong."

She was right. Pickings were slim around here, not that I was picking.

"Or I've done their taxes and know their bottom

line. You'd be surprised who shouldn't be driving around in an expensive SUV."

For college, I'd had a full ride scholarship. Everything was fully paid. I never liked living in the dorms, but I didn't turn down free housing in Boston. I worked as a math tutor to pay for food and incidentals. While I'd returned home broke, I didn't owe student loans either.

I got the job with James Corp and the inn project two weeks after I returned because I was qualified, and the position was hiring immediately. I'd been socking away the paychecks ever since. I wanted to move out as I was sure Lindy wanted her little sister out of the house after having it to herself for three years.

Looking back, I was sure she hadn't found a guy because of me. She'd been twenty-three when she became the mother to a ten-year-old. What guy that age wanted a tween to raise?

For now, and until we wanted to strangle each other–or she found a guy she wanted to bring home– I'd stay in my old bedroom.

"That's a good thing then," I told her, trying to give her dating challenges a positive spin. "You can screen out the over spenders before the first date."

"Hello!"

We turned toward the front door when Mallory called out. She came into the kitchen carrying a box of donuts from Deerdorfs, the local shop that was ah-mazing.

"I brought your favorites," she said, lifting the lid and grabbing her own favorite, a cruller with straw-berry glaze. She gave my sister a once over, then said, "Cute nightie, Lind."

"Thanks. I'm up three pounds. No way am I eating a Boston cream," Lindy said, crossing her arms over her chest as if to keep her hands away from grabbing one.

I had no such issues with weight or self-control. Besides, I ran this morning and could definitely use some sugar. I grabbed the one with the rainbow sprin-kles Mal had gotten for me and took a big bite. The donut dissolved on my tongue. Heaven.

"Did you figure out how to solve the problem from last night?" she asked me, arching a brow.

"What, a math problem?" I wondered, chewing the sugary confection.

"Right. *Math* problem."

Oh. *Oh.* She was talking about Maverick.

"Still working on it," I said, wanting to end the conversation. Until I had clear answers, and knew for a fact my job wasn't over, I wasn't sharing any of it with

Lindy. The last thing I wanted to do after what we'd just talked about was to be fired for inappropriate behavior. After dropping out of college, then that, Lindy would lose her shit.

I did get a side eye from her though. She might not be as crazy good at math as I was, she was an accountant and knew how to use a calculator. She also knew we were up to something, because knowing Mallory, we usually were.

"Go get ready," Mallory prompted, licking glaze off her lip. "The parade starts in thirty minutes."

"You're going to the parade?" Lindy asked, surprised.

I hadn't been in a couple years because I'd been in Boston and hadn't considered going this morning. I was now.

"You should come with us," Mal offered.

Lindy shook her head. "Work. Tax extensions. IRS letters."

While Lindy worked for a company in town as their in-house accountant, she also took on side clients. She worked all the time and carried her laptop around with her as if it were an extension of her body.

"We're going because Bridge is thinking about adopting a dog," Mallory commented, grabbing a napkin from the holder in the center of the kitchen table. I coughed because I sucked a sprinkle into the back of my throat. She'd practically grown up here, just as I'd spent tons of time at her parents' house and made herself at home. And made ridiculous comments like that one. A dog?

"What?" Lindy screeched, holding up her hands. "I don't think that's a good idea. The shedding alone will–"

Lindy liked dogs, but other people's. She'd raised me, so she'd done her time and had no interest in taking care of anything else. Although she did want kids. That she birthed herself, not stuck with when she was twenty-three... a year older than me now.

"I'm not getting a dog," I said, loud enough so she knew I was serious. "Mallory's being ridiculous."

"Well, I for one, want to see those dogs walking in the parade." She waggled her eyebrows at me.

I'd gone two whole minutes without thinking about Maverick James and she'd ruined it. Now I thought of him in that tight t-shirt. And him pressing me into the wall. Overpowering me but making me feel good. His mouth on mine, the hard length of him as I rolled my–

"Since when do you like dogs?" Lindy asked Mallory. "I thought your family loved cats. Don't your parents have two?"

Mallory nodded and took another bite of her donut. "Yes. Si and Am. Siamese cats like in *Lady and the Tramp.*"

We'd watched the Disney movie all those years ago and she'd begged her parents for the cats. Maybe that was where her overindulgent nature started. Maybe it was also where her obsession with things from movies began.

"I'll take a quick shower," I said, knowing I wasn't getting out of the parade and I needed to escape the kitchen before Mallory blabbed. If I argued, she might have said something about Maverick being in the Parade of Pooches.

"I'll have another donut while I'm waiting. Oh my God, this one is soooo good," Mal said with a mouthful of gluten, carbs, and sugar. "Come on, Lind, you know you can't resist."

"Oh, all right," was Lindy's reply as I shut the bathroom door.

13

MAVERICK

THE PARADE WAS a big deal in Hunter Valley. The group of us with the animal shelter were between the high school marching band and the scouts. Both sides of Main Street were filled with residents clapping, little kids ready to grab candy tossed from the various floats and well, probably everyone in the county. It was noisy, especially behind kids with instruments. The weather was amazing, sunny and not too hot. It was everything I imagined small town life to be like and I had to admit, I was completely sold. I was loving Hunter Valley more and more.

Montana wasn't always like this, I knew. I'd skied at

Hunter Mountain and there'd been snow piles lining the streets taller than me. For today? I'd enjoy the hell out of it. There were about thirty of us walking with shelter dogs, waving to the crowd, all of us in our pink t-shirts promoting the coffee shop.

My furry sidekick was Scout. Every time I looked down at him, I couldn't help but smile. He was a very obvious result of an Australian shepherd and a corgi getting together for a good time. He looked just like the sheep herding dog, only with legs five inches long. I would swear he smiled up at me, thrilled to be out of the shelter. He'd ridden in the passenger seat of my car to the start of the parade, head out the open window, taking in every scent that we drove past. He didn't need a leash, responding instantly to any command I gave. He sat, laid down, rolled over, fetched a ball, and even tried to herd me when I tried to step off the curb.

He was awesome.

There was no way in hell I was giving him back to the shelter.

It seemed I had a thing these days for wanting to keep the quirky ones.

Like Bridget, who I'd emailed last night. It was my first step to making things right and getting to kiss her again.

I'd like to think I'd have spotted her in the crowd due to a change in the Force or a spidey sense, but it was just too crowded. It was her friend Mallory shouting my name that had me turning.

Beside her was Bridget and fuck me, she stopped me in my tracks. A woman and a black lab mix cut around us. I apologized and moved out of the way, Scout following. As I approached, I took a few seconds to take in all five feet nothing of Bridget Beckett, my latest obsession. She wore shorts and a sleeveless top. Unlike the day before, her legs were bare. Her arms were bare. Her clothes fit her. While she might be small, every inch of her I could see–which was a lot– was toned and tanned. She had slim hips and small, high breasts I'd felt against my chest the night before. I knew her shape now and wanted to touch every inch of her. To memorize.

"Hi," I said, stopping right in front of her. Was it rude to ignore Mallory? Maybe, but she was ignoring us, having crouched down to pet Scout.

"Who's a handsome guy?" she crooned, rubbing behind his ears. "Yup, that big daddy up there sure is, but you are too."

Bridget tipped her head back to look at me and pushed her glasses up. Her cheeks flushed prettily and rolled her eyes.

I grinned because I couldn't decide who was more adorable, her or Scout.

Her. It was definitely her.

When her gaze flicked to the side, to whatever was passing in the parade behind me, then back, I couldn't miss how she was still nervous and wary. That hadn't changed.

It was as if she remembered everything about last night, from the feel of my dick beneath her hand to the fact that she was freaked about accidentally sharing the sex quiz.

"Hi," I said.

"Hi," she said back, then bit her lip.

It was obvious she hadn't seen my email yet, because if she read the attachment, she'd either slap me, jump me, or run away screaming. I knew which one I preferred but having her do none of them was also a win.

"What's the square root of three thousand, four hundred and fifty-eight?" I asked, picking a random number.

Her eyes met mine and she frowned. "Fifty-eight point eight. Why?"

My dick twitched at the fact that she answered that within a second. I had no idea if that was the correct answer, but I was sure she had it right. The number didn't care. I only wanted her to think of something, anything, besides her nerves.

I shrugged, studied the freckles on her nose. "No reason. Just wanted to hear your brain at work."

The corner of her mouth tipped up. "My brain's not that loud," she countered, remembering that we'd said the same thing at the coffee shop.

Fuck, she made me smile. I reached out–I couldn't help myself–and gave her bun a gentle tug. Yeah, I was definitely keeping her.

14

BRIDGET

How did he get better looking every time I saw him?

He had on the same ridiculous t-shirt that Eve gave him, but today it was paired with gray shorts and worn sneakers. His eyes were hidden behind a pair of aviator sunglasses. I knew he was a billionaire, but he didn't look it. Nor did he look like a corporate CEO. In fact, he blended in with the casual lifestyle of Hunter Valley. It almost seemed–besides the fist fight with Jason the day before–that it was relaxing for him to be here.

He even had a dog with him.

Mallory stood and brushed off her hands. "How's Theo?" she asked him.

If my friend's forwardness about his brother bothered Maverick, he didn't let it show. "I tried calling him this morning, but he didn't answer."

A group of gymnasts doing front walkovers and cartwheels passed in the parade. A mom or a coach pulled a wagon with a speaker that blasted the Olympics theme song.

"You were going to tell him about me, right?" she asked, raising her voice.

"Mallory, Jesus," I muttered. "Have you no shame?"

"None," she said proudly, lifting her chin, then grinning.

A piece of candy bounced off of Maverick's shoulder and he caught it, then handed it to a little boy standing on the curb beside us.

"Don't you have to keep up with the rest of the dogs?" I glanced at the parade and the gymnasts had passed a convertible with the town mayor sitting in the back was next. The shelter dog group was almost a block down.

He shrugged a broad shoulder, ran a hand over the back of his neck and looked down at the dog. He smiled and I would swear the dog smiled back at him.

"Nah. I'm keeping him so there's no reason to show him off."

"You are?" I asked. I couldn't imagine a dog fitting into his jet setting lifestyle.

"Awesome!" Mallory said, clapping her hands.

The dog gave a single bark of agreement, his small tail wagging. I'd never seen a dog like him before. He was clearly a mutt and put together as if someone had misassembled two different breeds. He was adorable and clearly attached to Maverick.

I didn't blame him. I wiped my mouth to make sure my tongue wasn't lolling out as I looked at him too.

"I've always wanted a dog," he admitted. "My father was too much of an asshole to have something that would bring joy to the house. My mother liked them well enough but wouldn't dream of getting slobber or hair all over the house. Four crazy boys was enough."

"Lindy, my sister, is like that, too," I admitted. "A clean freak."

He leaned down and petted the dog on the head. "The maids did the cleaning, but my brothers and I were hell to raise. Having a dog too may have pushed her over the edge. Now? It's the only grandchild, grandpet, grand anything she has, so she'll probably spoil him rotten."

"What's his name?" I asked, not wanting to delve into our family histories.

"Scout."

Scout cocked his head.

"He's thinking that we should go to lunch."

His dark doggy eyes were looking up at Maverick as if he was his new best friend. Knowing dogs, he probably did want something to eat. Still...

"Go with me, Bridget?" Maverick asked.

My mouth dropped open and I didn't know what to say.

"Oh look. There's Mary Jackson," Mallory said, pointing down the line of people at the curb. I looked that way but didn't see her parents' neighbor in the crowd.

My thoughts shifted. "You haven't liked that woman since the seventh grade when she yelled at you for cutting across her yard on your bike," I reminded, doubting the truth behind her words.

"What better time to make things right." She gave me a wink, then weaved around the kids snagging candy at the curb. "See ya, Maverick."

"She's a terrible friend," I muttered, watching her dart off. Intentionally.

"You sure about that?" he asked, offering me a small smile, as if he knew a secret. "I asked you to lunch. *You.* She left for you to do just that. What better time for me to make things right?"

I was all nerves, jittery as if I drank too much coffee.

He took off his sunglasses and tucked them into the collar of his shirt. Then, he leaned down to speak, although the parade and the crowd was too noisy for anyone to really hear us.

His dark eyes met mine and must've noticed my apprehension. "Your job is safe, Bridget. You're safe. With me."

I looked up at him, then worried my lip between my teeth. I didn't trust easily. Not with men. I liked Maverick. A lot. Too much for someone I met the day before. But there was something about him. Something different. Unique. I was drawn to him, and I didn't know how to stop. Not even after all that had happened. Did that make me reckless or fearless?

"You don't believe me," he said. A car horn tooted behind him and he didn't even flinch at the surprise sound. "That's okay. I respect that you're cautious. I'm proud of you for knowing your boundaries."

For some reason, that made me smile. His praise

didn't seem hollow and it made me feel good. "Really?"

I glanced at the curb and his fingers tipped my chin up. "Really. Have lunch with me. A picnic." He looked down at Scout. "You want a picnic, right?"

Scout woofed and neither of us could resist laughing.

I couldn't resist saying yes either.

15

MAVERICK

Before we grabbed lunch, Bridget guided me to a local pet shop and we began walking the aisles, collecting everything a new pet owner would need. We were in the dog food section comparing organic versus fresh meals in a refrigerated case. Scout was beside us, sniffing everything he passed.

"I have a feeling this dog's going to eat better than me," I said, reviewing the options. And their ridiculous costs.

Bridget pointed to a twenty-pound bag.

"Do you have a photographic memory?" I asked as I grabbed it, not paying attention to what it was and trusting her choice. I set it in the cart, and we moved further down the aisle.

She shook her head. "No, I just excel at STEM."

I eyed her, but she was studying the rawhide bones. She had to be downplaying her intelligence because it wasn't every day someone could do complicated math in her head. I couldn't imagine her knowledge being limited to only STEM–science, technology, engineering, and math–as she said.

She grabbed a smaller sized bone with knots on the ends and held it up for me to approve. I nodded, and she bent down to give it to Scout. After a quick lick of his lips, he took it and pranced down the aisle with it in his mouth, head up. He was fucking proud of that bone.

"You grew up here in Hunter Valley?" I asked, following, pushing the cart which now had the dog food, a collar, and doggie shampoo.

"Yes."

"Where did you go to college?" I found a set of stainless-steel food and water bowls and added them to the quickly growing pile.

"You didn't see it in my personnel file?"

She threw that out there to test me. To see how much info I'd dug up on her, if I'd been talking about her to HR.

I could've. I considered it, but whatever was in her paperwork didn't give me a picture I was getting now, here in the pet store.

"That's not the Bridget I want to know," I said.

"Oh," she replied, looking a little contrite. Her wariness was still showing, and it only pissed me off. If she'd only have read my email by now, I'd have eased her mind.

Maybe. Hopefully.

"I went to MIT."

I couldn't help but look surprised. "Wow. Impressive."

She glanced at me, then away. "What else do you think he needs?" The *he* she was talking about wasn't me, but Scout. I needed her, only too eager to be tossed scraps of her smiles and kisses. She couldn't see that through her own insecurities.

I had to fix that. I told her I would, but it seemed it was going to take time. Didn't she know she was dragging me around, the six foot plus guy, by the fucking balls?

I stopped walking and she turned back. I needed her to know how I saw her.

"Baby, why do you do that?" I asked.

A frown marred her brow as she cocked her head, met my eyes. "What?"

"Lessen your value."

"I'm not... That's–"

"You're a math genius," I said, cutting off anything she might say negatively about herself. "Probably an all-around one. You went to MIT. That's something to be proud of. Hell, I'm proud of you."

Her cheeks flushed and she looked down. Scuffed her sneaker across the floor. "Don't be. Trust me." Her voice was soft. Small, like she was trying to make herself that size.

"Why the hell not?" I asked, suddenly frustrated and a little angry. Why shouldn't I be impressed with her?

She sighed and glanced away. "It doesn't matter."

I waited for her to say more, to explain, but she didn't. When she finally looked up at me, she smiled, but it was totally fake.

"What else does Scout need?" she asked again. "A dog bed. He definitely needs a bed."

She spun on her heel and left me in the aisle. Confused. And more intent than ever.

I was going to figure out what was going on, like Scout with his bone. I wasn't giving Bridget up and I needed to move things along.

16

BRIDGET

"I SENT YOU AN EMAIL," Maverick said, once we'd put all of Scout's new things in the trunk and settled into his car.

The dog was in the back seat, pushing his head out the open window, bone in his mouth. He hadn't set it down since I handed it to him. I didn't know how long he'd been in the shelter, but if I'd been locked up like he had, offered freedom and a big treat, I probably wouldn't let it go either.

"Oh?"

Maverick pulled his car out of the parking spot, glancing over his shoulder as he did so. The windows were down and the warm air swirled around us. This had to be a rental, but it was more muscle than the usual loaner. Being CEO of a billion-dollar company, I assumed he didn't fly commercial to get here, so whoever arranged his travel arranged for this as well. His assistant, I assumed, who'd also shared his favorite sandwich for the meeting yesterday.

"Can you pull it up on your phone?" he asked, his gaze on the road.

"Yes. Is it about the report? We can go over the details over lunch." I shouldn't be surprised he wanted to work, even on a Saturday. I'd hoped that when he'd met with Ed and Bixby at the site the day before, he'd have gotten all his issues resolved. Obviously not. "If you want sandwiches, turn here and go down a block."

He drove where I pointed and within a minute, parked in front of my favorite deli. It was where I'd gotten lunch for the meeting the day before, but since the sandwiches were so good, I could eat them all the time.

After shutting off the engine, he turned in his seat, setting his forearm on the steering wheel.

"I'll get the food and you can read it."

I could only nod because he was my boss. If he wanted to work over lunch, then that was what we would do.

"Okay. Sure."

His eyes met mine. "Promise me, that whatever you read, you won't run. That you'll be here when I come back out."

A shot of worry had me panicking. Why would he ask that of me? "You're not firing me? I mean, you could just tell me, right? It doesn't need to be all official in an email." I asked, wondering if running was exactly what I should do. Except he'd had plenty of time to terminate my job already today and hadn't yet, but I still had to ask.

His eyes softened and so did his voice. "No, baby. I'm not firing you."

He reached up, stroked a finger down my cheek. Heat sizzled in the same path.

"You'll be here?" His dark eyes held mine as he asked.

I nodded and seemingly satisfied, he unfolded himself from the car.

I stared after him as he went inside. Scout hopped into the front and sat in the driver's seat. Watched out the window.

Grabbing my cell, I pulled up my work email, then scrolled through my inbox and opened the one from Maverick. He'd sent it last night.

. . .

Baby,

Now you have leverage over me. You can take this to HR at any time. While I do own the company, the board of directors can fire me. You can make a hefty settlement from using this.

I know your email was a mistake but what you wrote was the truth.

This is all true too.

Mav

I READ IT TWICE, then opened the attachment called Sex Quiz.

Who do you want to do it with?

Bridget Beckett

"Oh. My. God." It was a quiz just like the one I sent him, but it seemed he reorganized the questions so I knew right away it was about me. No, him and me. Together.

On a scale of 1 to 10, how kinky you are?

I'll do anything from sweet to wild. I can do slow all the way up to fuck her in front of others. If Bridget has a need, it's my job to meet it.

"Fuck me in front of others?" I whispered to Scout, who tilted his head toward me.

Dropping the bone on the seat, he hopped into my lap as if he wanted to read it with me.

"Oof. You are short, but you're not a little dog," I told him, shifting his body so his butt was by the window and not in my face.

Setting my hand on his furry back, I kept reading.

Now I knew why Maverick worried I'd run. This was unbelievably inappropriate for work, and I'd only read two answers. Fireable. And naughty. The kiss the night before had been one thing but learning about Maverick's darkest fantasies was hot.

So I pushed on. Duh.

What's the one thing you wish to get from your partner?

Everything. No holding back. I want to know every-thing about Bridget. What color her nipples are. Where she's ticklish. If she shivers when I lick the inside of her thigh. The sound of her moan. What she looks like when she takes my big dick for the first time. If it'll make her squirm.

Holy shit. I fanned myself because that was insanely hot and nothing the board of directors of James Corp should know about. That's why he sent it. This took *you show me yours and I'll show you mine* to a different level. I sent mine to him by mistake. He sent his to me on purpose.

What's your darkest fantasy?

I can't pick one. Bending Bridget over my bed as I wrap her hair around my fist. I'll fuck her from behind as I admire a green gem topped plug in her ass. Telling her she's a good girl for taking my dick so well and she'll spread her legs to take even more.

Um... what? Okay, maybe.

Watching as she tries to take all of me down her throat. Tears would well in her eyes because I'm too much but still opening wider because she knows I love it. Bridget climbing in my lap and working herself onto my dick. I'll watch her face as I cram her little pussy full. Too full that it hurts a little as my baby comes. Bridget sitting on my face and I suck on her aching clit as I finger fuck her until she screams, then squirts all over me.

Squirts? I couldn't even come for a man, let alone squirt. Could he do that? I wasn't sure about squirting, but he could definitely get me to squirm, because I was doing that right now.

Seeing her take off her cum soaked panties knowing she was covered in me all day... and asking me to be filled up with more. My baby on the kitchen counter, spread wide and–

The driver side door opened and I jumped. Maverick settled into the driver's seat, then leaned to the side and tugged the bone from beneath him. He tossed it in the back and Scout went after it, his little claws digging into my thighs.

Maverick set the bag of food at my feet but kept his dark eyes locked on mine. They couldn't hide how vulnerable he felt. This email was dangerous for him. Professionally, the email was suicide. Personally, he put it all out there. Unless he moonlighted as an erotic author, he really was sharing what he wanted to do with me. To me. For only knowing each other twenty-four hours, he'd spent a lot of time fantasizing. About me.

We could fuck or I could fuck him over.

He was leaving it up to me. Trusting me. Just as he wanted me to trust him in return.

It was a strange dichotomy, his intention versus his words. He'd made it so I wasn't embarrassed or ashamed, or worried my email mistake would affect my employment. He was a gentleman. Protective, even. But he wanted to put a plug in my butt and fuck me from behind. Not a gentleman.

"Baby?" he murmured, seemingly losing patience for me to make a decision.

"Why did you write this?" I wondered.

"Because you needed something to feel safe. If me admitting what I want to do with you will do that, then it's worth it."

I couldn't help but laugh. "You know that kind of doesn't make sense." I took a moment to think about it all. "You're not firing me. You're not mad that I sent the email. You laughed off the coffee spill and you're not mad that you have to stay in Hunter Valley since it was my fault Jason was fired."

He sighed and the muscles in his body relaxed. A big hand settled on my thigh, his palm on my bare skin, his fingers on my shorts. "Let's go down your list. I'm not firing you. I'm not mad about the email. Thank you for spilling coffee on me. If not for that, I wouldn't have the coolest dog ever."

I hadn't thought about that. Out of the corner of my eye, I saw Scout sitting in the middle of the back seat watching us.

"Yes, I'm staying in Hunter Valley," he continued. "Yes, it's because of Jason Jimenez. But it's not your fault he was fired. He was an asshole. A shit leader. A shit human. I don't employ men like him." His fingers squeezed gently. "You need to tell me what he said and did."

I frowned. "Like what?"

"You heard what he said to me. That locker room talk."

I swallowed. "Yeah."

"What else did he do?"

I shrugged, then looked out the window. "Wonder how I could be so smart and have such a nice ass. Things like that."

His fingers clenched, then he pulled his hand away to rub it down his face. "Did he ever touch you? Jemma?"

"No."

"Why didn't you report him?"

"Because I need my job, that it's his word against mine. Against Jemma's. I'm just his assistant."

"Right." He was angry. A blood vessel throbbed at his temple. "You did his work for him, too."

I licked my lips. Nodded.

"Even though he's already fired, on Monday, you and Jemma, and anyone else he fucked with, will file formal complaints with HR. Trust me, I'll make sure he doesn't find a job. Anywhere."

I believed him. The fact that he had the power and ability to protect not just me, but other women he would work with.

"You need to tell me if someone's bothering you. Whatever it is."

I give my head a slight shake. "You can't fight my battles."

"Like hell I can't. Look at me." He pointed to himself, but his finger tapped the words Steaming

Hotties on his pink t-shirt. "You think I'm not big enough to handle it?"

I laughed. "You can handle anything."

"There's one thing I'm struggling with," he said softly, glancing at the gear shift, then at me through his dark lashes.

"Oh?" He was powerful, successful, handsome and every other adjective I couldn't think of right now.

"You."

17

MAVERICK

I WANTED to punch Jimenez all over again for the way Bridget looked at me right now. Unsure. Her confidence dented. That was fucking wrong.

She was brilliant and beautiful and I wanted to make her see that. To believe it.

Any other woman who read my sex quiz would be naked and riding my dick by now. Every word of it had been accurate and I'd thought of Bridget, and only Bridget as I'd typed it out. The fact that she wasn't just clothed, but unsure, meant she wasn't a fling kind of woman. She didn't do casual.

Neither did I because if that was what I still

wanted–and I'd lost interest in that back in my twenties–I'd have gone to a bar and picked up someone. Fucked her. Left her. All of that and not learning her name. Was my age showing? Was that her holdup?

"Did you mean what you wrote?" she asked, a flush creeping up her neck.

My dick got hard, and I shifted in my seat. "Every word."

She was thinking. Sexy thoughts based on the way she bit her lip and wouldn't look me in the eye. I had to wonder what specifically.

"Did you like it?" I prodded.

She gave the slightest of nods and I wanted to reach into the back and high five the dog who was staring at us as if he were following along. I gave him a look and he went to the window and stuck his head out.

"Was there... was there something specific you liked the best?" I reached out, stroked her hair, leaned close so I could breathe in her sweet scent. "Be a good girl and tell me."

Her gaze lifted and... fuck. That. Right there. In those sparkling green eyes, eagerness that couldn't be hidden by her glasses. I hadn't asked her if she wanted to sit on my face. Or if she wanted to try to get my dick down her throat. No. I hadn't said anything but *be a good girl.*

That... those simple words had her running hot. It was what she meant in her quiz about her fantasy. Being on my knees. It didn't seem like it, but it all made sense and fuck, would I satisfy her. Because her making me happy made her hot.

She was a people pleaser. No wonder she didn't file a complaint about Jimenez. No wonder she wanted to make sure I didn't see the email, because sending it to a co-worker was wrong. She'd been bad in making the mistake and she'd tried to fix it so I wouldn't know about it. Wouldn't think she'd done something wrong.

She wanted to be a good girl. *Needed* to be.

And that made my dick ache because she was good. Perfect, even, in all her quirks and blunders. My chest swelled with pride.

"You want that, don't you?" I whispered, curving my palm around so it cupped the back of her neck. "To be my good girl?"

Her pink tongue flicked out and she licked her lips again. "Yes," she admitted.

Pre-cum soaked my boxers at her admission.

"Tell me then. What you liked best."

"I want... I want to sit in your lap."

The breathy way she said that... *fuck.*

"And slide down onto my dick," I finished for her. "Is your pussy wet, baby?"

I gave her neck a little squeeze and her eyes met mine. "Yes. Take me to your place so I can show you."

I groaned at her boldness. She didn't have to tell me twice.

18

BRIDGET

"This is amazing," I commented, taking in the house. It was situated at the base of Hunter Mountain, but on the west side, nowhere near the ski slope. That meant nowhere near other people. Towering pines were on either side of the log house and had views of the entire valley from the wall-to-wall windows at the back. A two-story river rock fireplace was along one wall with a plush sectional facing it. It could seat at least six, or one Maverick. It was professionally decorated with tans and blues and lots of wood. By the size, I assumed there had to be six or more bedrooms. Probably a walkout basement. All of it came with a hefty price tag.

"My assistant found it for me. It's better than a hotel."

"This is where you'll stay then?"

His cell chimed and he pulled it from his pocket, read the screen. His jaw clenched, but he didn't give whatever he read much thought because he set the phone and his car keys on the granite counter in the kitchen, then joined me by the window. Scout was sniffing around, checking out his new home.

"This is the first time I've been in it," he admitted. "After I knew I was staying yesterday, I got him to find me a rental. He texted me the address and the door code first thing. I drove by earlier to see where it is, but yeah, it seems nice."

Seemed nice? It was perhaps ten steps above *nice*. Twenty.

Taking my hand, he tugged me to the sofa, dropped on it, spread his knees wide and pulled me to stand between them. His hands cupped my hips and we were eye-to-eye.

"Hi," I whispered, suddenly a little nervous. We hadn't said much on the ride here from the deli, but the air had been charged. It had practically crackled.

I'd had sex before, but it hadn't been like this. The anticipation. The need.

I wanted him.

He wanted me.

I was wet and I told him so.

He was hard. It was impossible to miss. That bulge.

"Hi." A small smile tugged at the corner of his mouth. "Can you see without your glasses?"

I wasn't expecting the question. "Do you need me to drive anywhere?"

His lips twisted in amusement. "No."

"Then I'm good."

He reached up and carefully took them off, reached out and set them on the side table.

"Come here," he murmured, patting his thigh.

"Aren't I supposed to be naked?" I asked, referring to his quiz.

"Come here," he whispered.

I set one knee on the couch beside his thigh and straddled him. His hands went to my hips and pulled me closer so I could feel how hard he was against my center.

"There's my good girl."

A curl of lust rolled through me. Fuck, why did that do something for me? His praise, his hold. Sitting in his lap? It was like coming home, this feeling. Comfortable. Easy.

"I think we need to talk," he murmured.

I swallowed, suddenly nervous. My heart hammered and I couldn't hold his eyes. Whenever someone said *we need to talk,* it was never good. "I'm sorry, I–"

"Hey," he murmured, then tipped my chin back to his. His palm cupped my jaw. "What are you sorry for?"

"I thought you wanted to talk."

He angled his head, studied me. "So you assumed you did something wrong?"

Exactly, but I offered him a small shrug.

"Oh, baby. No. No, you're perfect."

I met his gaze now, not because he was holding my head in place. His gentle words had me relaxing and I knew he felt my body ease.

"I don't know what the hell this is between us, but I feel it," he admitted, his hands moving from my hips to gently coast up and down my thighs. "You feel it too, or you wouldn't be in my lap right now."

It wasn't worded as a question, so I didn't answer. Except he was right. I felt it, the tingling of need. The desire to be with him. To have him look at me, just the way he was right now. It was desire, definitely, but something more. Like he... *craved* me.

His touch warmed my skin. Awakened me better than caffeine.

"I held your hand at the coffee shop. I wanted to sit with you and talk. Get to know you. But you ran off. You ran off again last night."

I had. Both times.

"Whatever this is, it's not because of any email. I wanted you before I even knew who you were. We'd be right here, right now, if you sent your email to Mallory." His hands slid around my back, one drifted up my spine to cup the back of my neck. The other settled low to cup my ass.

"I'm a foregone conclusion?" I asked, licking my lips.

He shook his head, squeezed his fingers. "No, baby. *We* are."

There was a distinct difference and I really liked that he pointed it out.

"You wrote that a man never gave you an orgasm."

I shifted, tried to get up, suddenly embarrassed.

"Be a good girl and sit still."

This time, his words weren't as soft, but deep and low and commanding. I instantly stilled.

His hands began to roam again, now up and down

my sides, his thumbs brushing the swells of my breasts. His knees parted further, and my thighs widened. Because of our size difference, I was completely open to him, even fully clothed.

When he cupped me there through my shorts and panties, I startled at the heat of his palm, the intimacy of the touch. His other hand palmed my breast, then skated over to the other, pinching the nipple.

I gasped at the feel. His touch was potent. Gentle, but insistent. Roaming and touching as if he had to learn my body.

"I should get the names of any man who touched you so I can beat the shit out of them," he said. "Or thank them for being such shit lovers because I'll be the one to give them to you. That's not ego talking. It's my job now to satisfy you. Why? Because you climbed in my lap where you belong. I will give you whatever you want. It's my job to satisfy you. You'll come, baby. I promise."

Holy shit. I... I'd say he was a dirty talker, but it wasn't all that dirty. It was all promise. From a focused lover who only had one thing in mind. Me.

His hands continued to roam, caressing every inch of me. As if he couldn't stop himself. I was melting, like a smore over a fire, getting all gooey and soft.

Dripping, even. I had no idea over the clothes petting was so hot.

He leaned in, nuzzled his nose along my neck then whispered in my ear. "You just have to tell me how you want to do it. One question, multiple choice quiz. Do you want to come on my, A- Fingers; B- Mouth; C- Dick or D- All of the above?"

19

MAVERICK

SHE WAS SO FUCKING SWEET. And sexy as hell. My dick was going to have a seam line imprinted in it. I couldn't stop touching her. Her little shorts and t-shirt allowed me to see her body, feel her silky skin. I could do this all day, have her in my lap and just touch her over her clothes.

In the car, she'd been bold. Brave. Told me she was wet. Coming here, to this amazing house Bradley had found for me to live, made her shy. That was okay. I wasn't going to rush her. She was right here with me on all of this. The only difference was that my dick and my brain were in sync. Hers wasn't quite yet, but she was getting there.

She had a lot to lose if I was the asshole she expected me to be. So she'd sit in my lap all fucking day until she caught on that I was different.

I wasn't the selfish lover who neglected her. The asshole who'd made her doubt herself. The fucker who'd made her apologize even when she didn't even know what she did wrong.

Breathing in her scent, I kissed along her neck. I couldn't help myself.

"I..."

I pulled my head back and met her eyes. Without her glasses, they were so bright. A shimmery green, slightly dazed. There was a spray of freckles across her nose and color bloomed in her cheeks.

"What?" I stroked the ends of her hair, the silky strands sifting through my fingers.

Her gaze dropped to my shirt and she lifted a finger to trace over the lettering on my chest. "I want to come, but I don't want to decide."

"Hmm," I murmured, considering. Maybe she was worried about choosing wrong, that I wouldn't like the answer. That was impossible because mouth, fingers, or dick were all correct options. Still, it was an insight into her. Letting go, giving up the need to think or decide. That pretty head of hers must churn all the time. "You want me to take charge?"

She nodded, then glanced up at me through her lashes. So fucking pretty.

With her sweet consent given and a plan in place, I was energized. Fuck yes.

My mission was to get Bridget to come any way I wanted.

"Choice E it is then," I replied. "Take your hair down."

She blinked, expecting me to say something different. Reaching up to work the hair tie from her bun made her tits lift beneath her t-shirt. I couldn't resist cupping them and running my thumbs back and forth over her nipples. They hardened beneath my touch.

Her hair fell in soft tendrils over her shoulders, down her back and brushed my fingers.

"Fuck, baby. You should wear it down."

I rubbed the ends of a silky strand, imagined the dark curtain spread over my pillow.

Scout trotted over and nudged Bridget's thigh. She laughed and gave him a pet.

"If we're going to be roommates," I told him. "You can't be poaching my girl."

Scout looked up at me, tongue hanging out with happiness.

Bridget laughed.

"This one's mine. Go take a nap." I pointed toward the thick rug in front of the fireplace. We didn't pull his things out of the trunk yet, but he'd be just fine until we did.

Lifting his chin as if insulted, he turned and did as I said, circling three times before settling in, eyes closing.

"Where was I?" I asked, tucking my fingers into the hem of her shirt, slowly worked it up, meeting her eyes and ensuring this was what she wanted. When she raised her arms over head, I got the green light and stripped it from her.

Her bra was pale pink and simple. But was it fucking hot as hell because it was perfectly sheer, her nipples completely visible. There was no lace. No satin. No ribbons.

I groaned because... fuck me. Pre-cum spurted from my dick just looking at her.

"Take it off," I said, my voice husky and deep.

Reaching behind her, she undid the clasp, let the bra slip off her shoulders, then dropped it on the floor, forgotten.

Setting my big hands at her back, I pulled her in closer, bent my head and took one lush tip into my mouth. Licked and sucked at that hard tip.

Bridget cried out and her fingers tangled in my hair. "Mav!"

I kissed my way from one to the other. "That's right. Say my name."

With my mouth on one breast, I cupped the other, played with her nipple, then switched. Back and forth until she was squirming, riding my dick through our shorts.

"I bet you can come if I play with these beauties enough," I guessed, my voice deep and rough like sandpaper. "But there's more of you I want to explore. Up."

I gripped her hips and lifted her off my lap.

Standing before me, she was perfection. Her hair was wild and long, her eyes blurry with arousal. Her breasts were pink from my play and her nipples hard little raspberries, all slick from my mouth. I flicked open the button on her shorts, slid down the zipper. She took over, shimmying the cotton down her hips so they pooled around her ankles. Her panties matched her bra and was equally sheer. I could see she wasn't shaved or waxed bare, but had a trim little thatch of dark hair above pink pussy lips. And I could see a dark spot proving she wasn't just wet but soaked.

I growled, ran a finger over that drenched fabric.

"You are wet. That for me?"

I lifted my gaze from her panty covered pussy to her eyes. She bit her lip, nodded.

"Show me," I growled.

Her eyes flared and she pushed her panties down.

"Give me your foot." I patted my thigh and she lifted her leg and did as she was told. Undoing the laces on her sneaker, I pulled it off, then her sock. She set her foot back down on the wood floor, then switched. This time, when I was done, I held her ankle.

Shook my head, so she knew not to move.

"Look at you."

With her leg raised, I could see her perfect pussy. Glistening and swollen, her clit peeking out from full pink lips. I breathed in her sweet scent. My mouth watered to taste her. I set her foot beside my thigh on the couch so she was more stable, but still wide open. Settling my hand back on her hip, I cupped her pussy with the other. This time, there was nothing between my fingers and her sopping core.

"Fuck," I breathed as she startled. "Shh."

Like I had with her body, I stroked over her folds, spreading her wetness and circling her clit. I felt her stiffen, then wobble. This wouldn't do.

I lifted her so she was back on my lap straddling me once more, this time completely bare. I'd thank

Bradley later for the floor-to-ceiling windows so it was
nice and bright. I could see every inch of her pale skin.
Her upturned breasts, those dark curls that couldn't
hide her–*my*–pussy.

Setting my knees wide once more, she hovered.

"Better?"

She nodded, bit her lip.

"Look at you, my good girl. On my lap showing me
everything. Where was I?" With one barely there
fingertip, I circled her clit, then slid it inside her. Tight,
wet heat surrounded the digit. A clench of her inner
walls squeezed.

Fuck.

She looked at me eyes wide. "Mav," she said on a
shaky breath.

"Like that?" I was barely touching her, just my
finger slowly pumping in and out of her. Wet sounds
accompanied the small movement and we both knew
how much she liked it without her saying a word.

She set her hand on my shoulder and arched her
back. "More."

I loved that she told me what she wanted, so I gave
it to her. Pulling out, I slid my ring finger in beside my
middle one, stretching her wide. Fuck, she was tiny.
Tight.

My dick pulsed at the idea of trying to fit.

She groaned and I pressed deep, my palm rubbing her clit. Then she began to move, although only little rolls of her hips because she had no traction propped on my thighs. Her tits thrust up with every shift and with my free hand I began to play with them. Cup, knead, a gentle squeeze. Then a pluck and tug on a nipple. Switch sides.

She was going to come. That was my mission, and she was on her way there based on the sounds coming from her and the way she tried to roll her hips, but I wasn't sure if I could make it.

This sexy makeout/petting session was the hottest thing I've ever done with a woman and I was already close to coming.

I dropped my hand from her tits, opened up my shorts, reached in and pulled my dick up so it stuck out the top of my boxers in the V of space of the parted zipper. The relief was immediate, but so was the need to get inside her.

Bridget watched and then stared. My fingers were still deep inside her, but now still.

"You're big," she said, commenting on only what she could see of the throbbing head. There were inches and inches that hadn't been revealed.

A drop of pre-cum appeared at the tip and I swiped it with my thumb. Reaching up, I smeared it across her plump bottom lip, then pushed my thumb into her mouth. Her tongue swirled around it. I growled at the wet suck and I pulled it free.

She frowned.

"Keep doing that and I'll come all over myself," I warned.

She smiled, this time with a vixen's twist to her lips.

"This is all about you, baby. I want *you* to come all over my hand."

I slid my fingers up and down her front wall as I watched her face and knew the second I found her special spot.

"Mav!" she cried, her eyes wide with surprise.

Yeah, no one had taken care of my baby.

I curled my fingers right there. Her hips rolled and a moan slipped from her lips.

Concentrating on that spot, I got my other hand involved, resting low on her belly so my wet thumb circled her clit. It was slick and swollen and I watched as I pushed her right to the edge.

"Mav, Mav, please. I'm... I–"

Her head tilted back, eyes closed, but when she was close, her inner walls fluttered, a flush spread over her skin and looked to me, eyes wide and full of... panic.

So I talked her through it so she knew I was right there with her, that I had her. "Shh, such a good girl. You're going to come so hard. Your pussy was made for me. That's it. Let go for me. Yes. Fuck, yes."

Her gaze went blurry as she came, but she kept it locked on mine. Breathy little moans filled the room and the nails that she dug into my shoulder were going to leave marks.

Fuck me, I had a feeling she already had.

20

BRIDGET

Oʜ. My. God.

Oh my God.

That was... that... it, I... wow.

I blinked and I couldn't help the slow smile that crept across my face. My body was like taffy, pliable and soft. I felt amazing. Mav had rocked my world and it had been with his fingers. I could only imagine what it would–*will*–be like when he got inside me.

"Mav," I said, leaning back a little and then laughing with joy. Relief. Happiness. Pleasure.

He slipped his fingers from me, and I watched as he licked my wetness from them. I should be mortified by how wet I was, that pretty much his entire hand was covered.

But I wasn't, because watching him clean the fingers that had brought me to orgasm was unbelievably hot. He was virile, manly and probably really proud of himself.

He should be.

"I had an orgasm." My words were so darned happy.

"Yup," he said.

Lick.

"By a man."

"By me, baby."

Lick.

"That was..."

"It was."

Lick.

"I'm not done," he said, the determination in his eyes more like a vow than a statement.

"Good."

With a move too fast for me to do more than squeak, I was on my back sideways on the couch.

With a hand pressed into the leather by my head, he loomed over me. "I got a taste. Now I want it right from the source."

He shifted down my body, set one leg high on the

back of the couch, the other so it hung off the edge, then settled in between.

And went to town. And by town, I meant my pussy.

I'd never had a man go down on me before. I'd made out with a few guys in high school and college, but my professor was the only man I'd slept with. And I was quickly learning he was a very selfish, very *bad* lover.

Mav hadn't said anything about reciprocation and his dick was still–mostly–in his shorts. He wasn't in any rush to do anything but satisfy me.

When his tongue licked up my center in one long swipe, I pushed on his shoulders, then tugged on his hair. I was really sensitive from the first orgasm. "Mav!"

He didn't lift his head or stop, only looked up at me with those intense dark eyes and kept right on going. As if it was his mission in life to get me off. It didn't take more than a few seconds for him to do so because his tongue circled and flicked at my clit, then he sucked on it and that was it.

I arched my back, clamped my thighs around his ears and screamed.

21

MAVERICK

I WAS the only person to see her like this. To *make* her this way.

It was headier than taking over the company when my father died. More exhilarating than seeing my boutique hotel idea become reality. Hell, it was more amazing than becoming a dog owner.

"I'm not done," I warned, because I wasn't letting her out of my sight, or dressed, for the foreseeable future.

I sat back on my heel and wiped my slick mouth with the back of my hand. I knew what she tasted like now and I was addicted.

Bridget Beckett was like crack.

She hadn't moved since she came, her leg still thrown over the back of the couch–one I was probably going to have to replace, or immortalize.

"I did A," I told her. "And B. We're not stopping until we tackle C, which then means we'll have done D- All of the above. I fucking love doing a quiz together."

I hadn't kissed her in... too long, so I leaned down and took her mouth. No doubt she could taste herself because it was on my tongue. My lips. My skin.

It took awhile, but I lifted my head, then knelt above her.

There was that sly smile again and she looked up at me, relaxed and sated, not a self-conscious thought in her head. "If we're doing C, does this mean I get to see more than just the tip?"

Her gaze dropped to my dick. I pushed down the boxers and it sprang free. Gripping the base, I squeezed firmly, then stroked from root to tip. "Baby, you'll get more than just the tip."

Using her elbows, she pushed up, then came to her knees. "Can I?" she asked, biting her lip and having her hand hover between us.

"You can do anything you want. But not here."

I leaned forward, tossed her over my shoulder and

headed in the direction I assumed was a bedroom. I didn't care if it was the master or not as long as there was a bed. She giggled and I slapped her ass.

She froze, then wiggled.

"Again," she said.

Holy shit, she liked it.

I gave her another playful swat because I liked it too.

"Naughty girls get spanked."

I dropped her on the bed and as she bounced, I reached behind my neck and tugged off the t-shirt, let it drop to the carpeted floor. From her sprawled position on the bed, she eyed my torso like she wanted to get her hands on it. Then her gaze dropped to my dick which curved up toward my navel from the opened zipper. It was so hard it was almost painful. Pre-cum smeared across my stomach. Reaching into my boxers, I gripped it at the base, squeezed hard to hold off the need to come all over her bare skin and mark her. Maybe I should do that, take the edge off. Then I'd be ready to fuck her for hours.

Stroking from root to tip, I set one knee on the bed so she could do whatever the fuck she wanted when the doorbell rang.

Her gaze shifted to the open bedroom door behind me, alert. Distracted, which pissed me off.

"Whoever it is will go away," I said.

It rang again. Then once more immediately after.

Fuck.

"Stay here," I said, carefully tucking my dick back into my boxers and wincing as I worked the zipper up. Fuck the button.

After closing the door behind me, I stalked through the house, Scout circling my ankles, and threw open the front door, ready to tell off the religious cult or tree trimming service. Instead, I found my brothers. All three of them.

22

BRIDGET

WHEN MAVERICK DIDN'T COME BACK RIGHT away–which to me, bare-assed naked was thirty seconds or less–I ripped the bedding apart and wrapped the top sheet around me. Going to the door, I opened it a few inches.

Maverick was talking to someone. In the house from the sound of it.

"Bradley called me last night," the man who rang the doorbell said. I knew this because it wasn't Mav's voice. "Recommended I fly up here and see what the fuck was up."

"He said that?" Maverick asked.

"He left *fuck* out, but yeah."

"Why?"

"Because he's worse than a virgin's chaperone all up in your business."

"I didn't mean why he didn't say fuck," Maverick snapped. "Why are you here?"

"Farrah called him. Told me to tell you to call her."

"You're not here because of that."

"No, but I wanted to tell you before I forgot. He sent us because of some email."

Maverick swore long and thoroughly.

I didn't know who Farrah was, but I couldn't linger on that. An email? Every bit of orgasmic satisfaction was worn off and apprehension was kicking in.

"Hey, who's this guy? Hey, buddy."

A loud bark from Scout was followed by laughing.

"That's Scout, my new dog," Maverick explained.

"What?"

"You got a dog?"

That was two different guys asking questions. Not one, but two men had been at the door.

"Yes," Maverick replied.

"What the hell's up with his short legs? I thought Border Collies were taller than this."

"I think his father had an affair with a Corgi," Maverick explained.

More laughter.

"You got a dog and Bradley sent us up here because of an email? What the hell, Mav?" That was *another* male voice, so there were three of them. None of them sounded like they were selling something or planned to leave.

"Bradley is too efficient. He went through my inbox," Maverick told them.

Oh. My. God. Even though I was naked, I started to sweat. Bradley was his assistant and he read his work emails. That meant–

"So?"

"So he... wait. What the hell are *you* doing here?" Maverick shouted at one of them.

"Me? I'm your brother, too. Clearly you need us here if you got a dog. Hey, Scout. Who's a good boy?"

The third male voice that went from sarcastic to sweet. It seemed all three of them loved dogs.

"You work eighty hours a week in an operating room," Maverick countered. "Since when do you have time off?"

"Since Silas called me," countered the one who was obviously a doctor.

"Don't look my way." It sounded like the third brother and I pictured him holding his hands up in front of him. "You know it's the off season. The boys want to head to Montana to see our fucked up brother? I'm in."

No, there were four of them out there. From their banter, they were familiar with each other. I had to assume they were his brothers. The James brothers, the ones from the laptop photo Mallory drooled over.

"I got a dog. How is that fucked up?"

"Not the dog. He's pretty cool. It's the fact that your assistant thought you needed an intervention."

"Where the fuck's your shirt?" one of them asked.

"I was getting undressed when you rang the doorbell. Over and over," Maverick countered and I felt my cheeks flame.

He hadn't mentioned that he had a woman here, but why would he now? They were here because Maverick's assistant read his work emails. Clearly, it was part of his job to maybe screen them for Maverick. Answer less important ones for him, delete unnecessary ones. Read some for crazy women trying to sexually harass him.

I turned and leaned against the wall while holding the sheet around my chest. Had the assistant read *my* email?

Of course he had. It was the biggest red flag for a CEO and clearly found it–me–a problem. Enough to call in the second-in-command at the company to look into it personally.

I closed my eyes.

This... thing wasn't me and Maverick now. It wasn't our little secret. He'd said he'd fix it and he had, by sending me his own sex quiz, but that had been when it was only the two of us involved. Obviously, mine wasn't private any longer.

"Fine, you're all here," Maverick snapped. "Because Bradley does his job too well. You saw the email then."

Maverick sounded grim, nothing like how he talked to me.

"Fuck, dude. That's serious shit."

I had no idea which brother spoke, but it didn't matter, not when I heard a whistle of agreement from someone else.

They knew about the sex quiz! They'd read it. Thought it was *serious shit.* I thought the mortification last night was bad, but this was worse, which I thought wasn't even possible.

I was naked.

In Maverick's house.

Once they saw me, the brothers were going to find me and think I was a slut, or worse, a power hungry gold digger.

"It's none of your fucking business," Maverick growled.

"Not going to argue with you there. That was TMI," another brother said. "Look, I got off an overnight on-call shift and flew up here. I need a shower, then some golf. A hike. Something outside since I don't think I remember what fresh air feels like."

The doctor brother, I assumed.

"Fine. Follow me. You can crash in bedrooms upstairs."

Four big men were heavy and loud, so it was easy to follow their path up the steps and moving around upstairs.

Now was my chance. I had to get the hell out of here before they saw me.

It was one thing to read a sex email from a random, faceless woman. It was another to find her naked in their brother's house. If that wasn't enough... shit! My clothes were in the other room.

If they saw them, they wouldn't think I had stripped them off to take a shower. Not in front of the couch and tossed randomly about. It would be obvious what we'd been up to.

His three brothers were here to make sure Maverick didn't get involved with me because it seemed not only did they care about him, but his assistant was ruthlessly protective to send them all this way.

I opened the bedroom door and tiptoed down the hall, then dashed to the couch with the sheet whipping around my ankles and started picking up my clothes. Shorts, t-shirt, sock, sneaker.

A throat cleared and I leapt in the air. Stifled a scream. Then froze.

Shit. *Shit!*

Sitting in a leather chair by the fireplace was one of the men from Maverick's laptop background photo. This one wasn't Theo, if Mallory's obsession and his attractiveness from the photo was correct. It was the one who looked the most like Maverick. Same dark hair and eyes, but he had a neatly trimmed beard. His elbow was on the arm rest and dangling from his finger was my bra.

The grin made me hate him. The fucker was enjoying himself. If the others came back...

Whipping my head around, I glanced up the stairs.

No sign of Maverick or the other two. I ran over to the brother, snagged the bra, then bolted. I wasn't staying here a second longer to get dressed. I could do it behind a pine tree or something where I was alone. If a neighbor saw me–which I doubted since the multimillion-dollar price tag on the house ensured privacy–it wouldn't be any more mortifying than being caught by one of his brothers.

Maverick drove and I had no way of getting home, but I was a runner. The distance back to town was less than what I did for my workout earlier this morning. I opened one of the glass doors out onto a stone patio and took off, holding my clothes close to my chest with one hand and the bottom of the sheet up off the ground with the other.

23

MAVERICK

My brothers were the biggest bunch of cockblockers. I was a minute away from sinking inside a sated, uninhibited Bridget and they rang the fucking doorbell.

I should be thankful for Bradley's diligence at his job and concern for my well-being, but sending Silas, Dex, *and* Theo? That was a little much. I was thirty-seven years old, not seventeen.

If I wanted to look on the bright side, he didn't send our mother. But he knew that would have been a fireable offense because she meddled enough trying to get grandchildren out of us. She'd divorced our asshole father years ago and had lived well off the revenge-money she'd gotten out of the settlement. Where he'd been a selfish prick, our mother was a saint.

After pushing Theo and Dex into the first two bedrooms I found, I turned around and headed back downstairs. I wanted to introduce Bridget to them, to show her off like Scout was proud of the dog bone. They'd like her, find her as unique and amazing as I did. Except she was mine and they could find their own brilliant, sexy woman. They'd meet her. Dressed, would be good. Her clothes were all over the place by the couch. That had me thinking of stripping her bare and I was pissed all over again.

My dick wasn't all too happy either.

Silas stood by the windows looking out at the view. "Um... I just handed a very pretty, very *young* woman her bra."

I narrowed my eyes and glared. He held Bridget's bra? Meaning she hadn't been in it when he met her? "What the fuck?"

He raised his hands. "Whoa, just saying."

I spun in a circle, took in the fact that Bridget's clothes were missing, then headed toward the downstairs bedroom to tell her what was going on. That our little Saturday afternoon fuckfest was postponed and, while my balls were going to be fucking blue, I was eager to show her off. I'd spoken briefly to Silas about her the day before right after meeting at the coffee shop, but so much had happened since then.

"She's not in there," Silas called.

I stopped, turned around again. He was pointing out the window.

"I think we may have scared her off." Then he winced. "Naked."

The idea of Silas seeing Bridget's perfect body had me losing my shit.

"What the fuck?" I said again, this time a few decibels louder.

I stormed over to the window and caught sight of Bridget sprinting across the open field to a pocket of ponderosa pines. A white sheet was wrapped around her and flowed out behind her like the hem of a long dress.

"Jesus Christ, Si. Why didn't you stop her?" I opened the door and ran after her. "Bridget!"

For a little thing, she was fucking fast and disappeared into the greenery.

I followed, grabbing one of her socks that she'd dropped on the way.

"Bridget," I called again, weaving through the grove of trees. Branches were low to the ground so once surrounded by them, I could barely see the field or the house. I followed the rustling and found her with her shorts on and working her bra straps over her shoulders.

She wasn't crying, but she was freaked. Bright spots of red were on her cheeks. Her skin was dotted with sweat and her eyes were angry and wild. For running so fast, she wasn't breathing all too hard.

I was.

"Baby, stop."

Ignoring me, she fought with her bra even more at my words, finally getting it to clasp.

Earlier, I'd barely had time to take in her long hair, but like this, it was wild and dark over her shoulders. Her chest rose with her ragged breaths.

"Where are your glasses?" I asked. While I was riled, I tried to keep my voice calm.

Her shoulders slumped and she ran a hand over her face. "They're by the couch. Shit."

I grabbed the t-shirt off the ground at her feet, turned it right-side out and handed it to her. I loved seeing her in that peekaboo bra, but now wasn't the time. I wanted her covered and safe. Reassured because she'd been spooked enough to bolt. "Why did you run?"

"Why did I– Are you serious right now?" she

shouted, staring at me as if I asked her if she thought the earth was round.

A bird squawked overhead. In the shade of the tall trees, it was cooler, but I was sweating.

"I want you to meet my brothers. They showed up unexpectedly."

She shook her head. "No way. I'm going home."

"I'll take you home, but I want you to meet them first."

"Why?" she snapped, but the hurt look in her eyes said she was more wounded than angry. "So they can laugh at me since they know my sex secrets? So they can do your assistant's work and tell you to steer clear of a woman who sends a guy a sex quiz?"

Fuck. She'd overheard. Me talking with three men she didn't know. While she was naked.

It had boys-will-be-boys overtones of Jimenez from the stupid meeting the day before, where she'd left the room and he'd talked about how fine her ass was. Laughing as he did so.

I clenched my molars together, angry that not only had Bradley read her quiz, but my brothers knew about it.

No, worse. Shit.

They'd said they read it and it was TMI. Too much information.

No wonder she'd run off. Shame wrapped around her more thoroughly than the sheet had. It was a repeat of the night before, but so much worse. I understood now, could see how cruel it was and how the words hurt her.

I was so fucking big and it hadn't been my size that scared her off.

"Baby," I whispered, taking a careful step toward her.

"You should have just fired me," she admitted. "HR at least would have been diplomatic. Your brothers are here because they think I'm a stalker or sex crazed woman who wants you for your body and came to Montana to get me as far away from you as possible."

"You're not fired," I said. "We won't go over that one again. As for my brothers, I promise you that if they think you're a sex crazed woman who wants me for my body, they'll leave and let us get back to it."

A stick snapped beneath my heel as I closed the distance between us.

She was skittish but held still.

"That is *not* funny," she countered. "I took my bra from one of them and I was in just a sheet!"

"You already used me for *your* body," I reminded her. "You rode my fingers. Wiggled your pussy all over my mouth and you were about to use me for my dick."

She rolled her eyes and her cheeks flushed the same color pink as her nipples.

"As for you being sex crazed," I pushed on, "as long as you're sex crazed with me, I'm fucking fine with that."

I got close enough to wrap her in my arms, to feel her shaking. I cupped the back of her head, held her against my chest. This felt so fucking right, having her in my arms, trying to soothe her. Yet I hated that she was so upset.

I thought my attempt at wit and self-deprecation would make her feel better, but her next words slayed me. "Your brothers read my sex quiz. Nothing you say is going to make that better."

Fuck. She was right. I didn't give a shit what my brothers thought. It was what they knew.

I told her I would fix this, me getting her email and what it meant to others.

I had. Or I thought I had.

Then I went and blew it all over again.

24

BRIDGET

Out of all the things I imagined doing with Maverick–and I'd thought of a lot–hugging him wasn't one of them. But even angry and upset, it felt amazing. Maybe it was that good *because* I was angry and upset. I couldn't remember the last time I'd been hugged. Held like this just for the sake of being comforted.

I couldn't be mad at Maverick. It wasn't his fault. The fact that his assistant read my email and then shared it with Maverick's brothers was a result of my mistake. The person who was the hardest on me was myself. Rightfully so. I'd made a stupid, stupid mistake and the fallout was growing.

He was trying to make it better, to make me feel better, when it wasn't his job to do that. Maybe that was why I clung to him a little more. And realized he wasn't wearing a shirt. My bra-covered chest pressed into his bare one. Even though he'd had his head between my thighs–holy shit that had been amazing– this was the closest skin on skin we'd gotten. Against my cheek, he was smooth and warm, but beneath, he was muscular and solid. A smattering of chest hair tickled my nose.

His scent was stronger this close. Some kind of woodsy soap. Or could be soap combined with the fact that we were actually in the woods.

"I'm sorry," I said, trying to step back.

"Stay. Just a little longer," he murmured, softly stroking my hair, then kissing the top of my head.

"I shouldn't have run," I admitted against his bare chest. "I need to face this. It's my fault."

His hold loosened and I stepped back.

"Your fault? That my brothers are here?"

"I sent the email. I did this to myself."

"Fuck that," he said, his gaze dropping to my breasts.

I took him in all broad, bare chested and the button on his jeans was open.

He grabbed my shirt from my fingers and fiddled

with it so it was all bunched up and worked the open neckline over my head. "Those three are meddlers. They're not here because they want to protect me from you." He gave me a heated look, as I tucked my arms into the short sleeves and he pulled it down my body, as if dressing a child. "Maybe Bradley's concerned, but I'm a big boy. They're here because Bradley clued them in that I was acting strange because of a woman, therefore they're curious about you."

"Me?" I asked, pointing at my chest. "That's laughable, especially if they read the quiz."

Using one finger, he tipped my chin up so I had no choice but to meet his dark eyes. "Baby, what did I say would happen if you talked about yourself like that again? Hmm?"

I swallowed. He said he'd spank me.

"Shit. Based on the way you're looking at me right now, and how you asked for more earlier, spanking your ass a pretty shade of red isn't going to be much of a punishment." His finger shifted to tuck my hair back behind my ear.

He was probably right.

As if he couldn't help himself, he leaned down and kissed me.

It was heated, but quick.

He stepped back, snagged my hand. "Come on. No

matter how much I want to, I'm not fucking you in the woods. My brothers are harmless. They're not assholes. I promise, whatever teasing they do, it'll be at my expense. Not yours."

I couldn't stay in the pine trees forever and Mav wasn't letting me run home. "Okay."

He turned around and gave me his back and crouched down. As he looked over his shoulder, he said, "Climb on."

I laughed. "What? You're going to give me a piggyback ride?"

"You only have one shoe. Besides, this way I know you won't run off again."

25

MAVERICK

I WASN'T KIDDING when I didn't want Bridget running off. Again. She bolted from the coffee shop. From the office the night before. And now.

Enough running.

I was going to end this sex quiz email shit once and for all and I needed her to agree that it was fixed.

There was no way to make my brothers or Bradley forget what they read in her quiz, but like I told Bridget, they weren't assholes and would treat her with respect. If they didn't, they would after I broke their noses.

When I went back in the house, I found the three of them sitting at the kitchen island.

"That was our lunch," I said, spotting Bridget's glasses where I'd left them next to the couch. I grabbed them and handed them to her over my shoulder as I went into the kitchen and set her on the counter by the deep farmer's sink.

"You weren't eating it," Dex said with his mouth full, eyeing Bridget with surprise.

I leaned against the counter right next to Bridget, not leaving her side. Scout came over, nudged my shin with his nose. I leaned down to stroke his ear.

"That idiot is Dex," I told Bridget.

"What?" he asked, licking a dollop of mayo off his lip. "I'm a growing boy."

"He's twenty-seven, not seven, although it's hard to tell."

He grinned and preened under the sarcasm and gave Bridget a wink.

I glared.

"The one eating all the chips is Silas." He offered her a little wave. "The other is Theo." I pointed at both of them.

"Silas and I kinda already met," Bridget said, her voice soft.

I glared his way next, knowing he'd held her bra.

"This is Bridget Beckett," I said, setting my hand on her knee.

Three sets of eyes followed the action, although based on the fact she'd run from the house in just a sheet they knew there was something going on between us. Something naked.

She offered a little finger wave, her glasses perched back upon her nose.

"I guess you never got to do that fantasy in the email," Silas commented.

Bridget gasped and I lost my shit. I was beside him in two steps and had him hoisted off the stool before he had a chance to react. It slid across the hard wood, then tipped over with a loud clatter.

"Hey!" he shouted as I shoved him against the wall. "What the fuck?"

I heard the slide of the other stools, Dex and Theo standing. Scout barked.

"That was uncalled for," I growled and gave him a shove, even though there wasn't anywhere for him to go. "Apologize to Bridget. Now."

I was right in his face and his eyes were wide with shock. I didn't usually go off like this, especially with him, but he also shouldn't be disrespectful.

"I'm sorry, Bridget," he said, looking in her direction. "But for what? I mean, you wrote all sex stuff in a fucking email and I was messing with you." His eyes, dark just like mine, shifted to me. "I didn't take you for a butt plug kind of guy. Too uptight."

"Si's right," Dex said from behind my back. "I'm not into knowing what you do with your dick, but your email was like reading a bunch of romance novels. Bridget, if he does half the stuff he wrote, you're going to have some fun with my older brother."

I let go of Silas and stepped back.

"Wait. You read *my* email?" I asked, setting my hands on my hips.

Silas adjusted his shirt, then gave a lazy smile. "Yes, your email. Bradley sent it to me first thing this morning. He figured since you sent something like that to an employee–which is completely unlike you–it was like a secret message saying you'd been kidnapped and needed help. I called Dex and Theo to come along and rescue you."

"Clearly he doesn't need rescuing," Theo said, his voice deadpan.

"Why do you need to write that shit down?" Dex asked. "Just do it like everyone else."

Theo chuckled. "It's been a while for him," he told Dex, referencing me and my sparse dating history. "Maybe he had to write it down to remember. He is old."

All three of them laughed and I glanced at Bridget.

This, I could take. I didn't give a shit that they were making fun of me. She was smiling, somehow enjoying the stupid banter. I went over to her where she was still perched on the counter and settled right in front of her, set my hands on her thighs. Just touching her calmed me.

"They read *my* email," I said, confirming she was following along.

She nodded, tucked her hair back.

I met her green eyes but spoke to the guys. "Bradley only sent you that one email?" I asked them.

"You wrote her more than one?" Silas asked. "If it involves animals or how you like to be pegged, I'm out."

I took a deep breath, rolled my eyes, but focused on Bridget.

"They don't know about mine," she whispered.

I shook my head and leaned in close, my nose brushing over her ear. "They wouldn't say any of this shit if they knew how it all started. I think you deleted yours before Bradley saw it. Maybe he was eating dinner." I shrugged, having no idea, but was relieved... no, thrilled, mine was the only one he found.

"Yeah."

"Earlier, when I answered the door and you overheard, it was my email they were talking about. Not yours. They're here to give me shit. Nothing to do with you. You good now?" I asked, pulling back so I could meet her eyes. My thumbs stroked over the tops of her thighs. I couldn't resist touching her.

She lifted her hand, cupped my jaw. I tilted my head, kissed the palm.

"I'm good," she said, no longer whispering.

Thank fuck.

"I want to get rid of them and get back to what we were doing," I said.

"We can hear you," Dex said, the words garbled because he was eating again.

"You're not getting rid of us, so go put a shirt on," Silas added. "Sorry, Bridget."

I winked at her, then went to get that shirt off the floor in the bedroom.

When I came back, she was perched on a stool between Silas and Dex, eating a section of sandwich and laughing at something Dex was saying.

"–as a businessman. And he held out a briefcase to put the candy in. Didn't Farrah go as your secretary?"

He was talking about Halloween and me dressing up for trick or treating. I'd forgotten Farrah had done that.

"Who's Farrah?" she asked, popping a barbecue flavored chip in her mouth.

"I grew up with her. Our parents are friends."

I caught Silas's look, but I wasn't doing anything wrong. Farrah wasn't anything more than a friend, no matter what he heard. I knew it. Farrah knew it. That was all that mattered.

"You weren't even born when I did that," I told Dex, reminding him that he was young as hell. Then I glanced at Bridget, who was even younger.

Five years younger.

Shit. I'd been in high school when she was born.

The guys caught on too but didn't comment.

"What I don't understand is why you wanted to be like Dad," Dex continued.

I reached between him and Theo and snagged a section of sandwich from the counter. I'd bought several subs at the deli because I didn't know what Bridget liked. With three extra mouths to feed, I was glad I did that.

"Because I didn't know then how much of an asshole he was."

"Our father was a dick," Silas explained.

"Is your father a dick?" Dex asked. "I bet he's not. You're really nice, although there's probably something wrong with you if you're into Mav and not me. I'm younger. Cuter, too."

"Jesus, Dex," I muttered, going around the counter and leaning against it. They were using the four stools.

Bridget gave Dex a little eye waggle and a playful grin. "No. You're right. My dad was a nice guy."

We all picked up on the past tense. "Did he pass away?" Theo asked, using his soothing doctor voice.

She nodded. "When I was ten. My parents died in a car accident."

"I'm sorry, baby," I said. I went around to her, scooped her up and hugged her close. There was nothing I could do to make it better, but she'd know I would comfort her. For a stunned moment, she was stiff in my hold, then she relaxed and hugged me back.

The guys offered murmurs of agreement.

I finally let her go, when all I wanted to do was toss her over my shoulder again and carry her off to some quiet, non-brother filled room. But I didn't. I set her back on the stool and gave her room.

"Our father's dead too," Dex told her, as if he was telling her he also liked mustard.

"Did you get hit in the head during practice?" I asked. He had zero tact, but it had turned the conversation off of Bridget's parents' deaths.

"It's the off-season," he reminded. His summers,

besides working out to stay in shape, were his own. But when training camp started in September, his life belonged to his team.

"Don't listen to anything he says," Silas told Bridget. "He plays professional ice hockey and obviously got hit by a puck a few too many times."

"Wow. Which team?" she asked.

He told her and they started up a conversation about the sport. Silas looked over at me, then stood and started searching the cabinets. He found where the glasses were and filled one from the dispenser in the fridge door.

I followed him with a glass of my own. "I know what you're thinking," I whispered.

"What, that those two are better matched?" he whispered back.

"Scout's less of a puppy than he is," I replied. "She doesn't need a puppy."

No, she needed someone to give her gentle guidance. Reassurance. Orgasms.

Silas glanced at Dex and Bridget, how Dex was waving his arms around talking about carrying the Stanley Cup trophy, with Theo listening on, amused by our little brother's antics. I was ridiculously proud of Dex. We'd known he'd play professionally when he was ten and carried his PeeWee team to state champs. He just had that ridiculous innate talent and was drafted out of college in Minnesota because of it.

"She doesn't look at him like she looks at you," he replied.

Bridget's eyes widened and she laughed at Dex, then put her fingers over her lips. He had a knack for making any story sound exciting.

"How's that?"

"Like he's her brother and you're her–"

"Don't even say it," I prompted. "I'm not that fucking old."

He shrugged. "Fine. Doesn't matter anyway. Daddy kink wasn't on your quiz."

Definitely not. Based on her response to the praise I doled out and being called a good girl, it made sense she was into someone so much older. Learning about her parents... I didn't think she had a Daddy thing either. But she did crave reassurance. Affection. Approval.

Dex couldn't give her what she needed, that was for fucking sure. He was too young for her, too into himself to pay close enough attention to her subtle tells. I saw them all and was working on responding to them correctly. It seemed in the past day I fucked up. A lot.

But she was here in my house, and she was meeting my brothers.

A big deal for a first unofficial date.

"I want to know what was on her quiz," he said, pulling me from my thoughts.

I growled, backed it up with a glare, then said, "Only if you want to die."

"So there really is one," he added. He played me and got the answer he wanted. The fucker. "I figured as much. You wouldn't share that shit in an email without a very good, and strategic, reason."

"I just didn't expect Bradley to be so good at his job," I muttered.

I would make sure he only worked regular business hours from now on so I could fuck up without anyone knowing.

26

BRIDGET

"WE WENT to the pet store to get things for Scout, then got deli sandwiches, didn't end up eating them because Maverick ate me and then his brothers interrupted because they read his email and I ran off in a sheet but it turns out they read Maverick's sex quiz and not mine and we're going out to dinner later and I need your help picking an outfit."

I didn't take a breath when I blurted all that to Mallory after Maverick had dropped me at home. Since I sprinted across a field barefooted and pretty much naked, I needed shower and a change of clothes.

"Hang on. Hang on," she said. "I have questions. Many questions. First one."

"Yes?"

"Theo is in town and you're going out to dinner with him?"

That was what she got out of my word vomit? One photo of the guy and she wanted to marry him.

"Yes."

"Can I come?"

I stood in my bathroom, looking at myself in the mirror. My hair was snarled from making out and then my mad dash. I had dirt on my cheek and... holy shit, was that a hickey on my collar bone? I tugged down the neckline of my t-shirt for a better look.

Yes, it was.

I grinned. Maverick had marked me.

Why I liked that, I had no idea.

"Yes, you can come."

"Next question, and I want to make sure I heard you correctly. Maverick wrote a sex quiz?"

"Yes."

"I have sub-questions about that, but I need to stay focused. Did you say Maverick *ate* you? Jake Ryan ate your pussy."

"He's not Jake–" I closed my eyes, then said, "Yes."

Her scream had me pulling my cell from my ear.

"I'll be right over."

She hung up and I hopped in the shower.

By the time I was done, Mal was pulling clothes from my closet. Her long hair was half up, half down in a cute look. She'd changed since the parade, and now wore a pale blue sundress that bared her shoulders and made the color of her eyes pop. She had on makeup and earrings. She was ready for dinner with zero notice, and I had no idea how she did it.

I went to my dresser for panties and a bra. When Lindy first took me and Mallory bra shopping when we were twelve, she told me to always get pretty matching bra and panty sets because no one was going to see them but me and it made a girl feel pretty. She said it was one thing to be pretty for others, with fancy clothes to show off in, but another to be pretty in secret.

Obviously, the talk was when I was young and years and years away from any boy ever seeing me in my underwear, but her lesson then made sense. I didn't have to make myself pretty for any guy. I hadn't. Not even for Professor Diego.

Until Maverick. For him, I wanted to.

"Why are all these things so big?" she asked, studying a black long-sleeved top I wore to work.

"Because my boss was a pervert, and I wasn't offering him a free show."

She lowered the shirt she held and cocked her head to the side. "That's fucked up all around. None of your clothes are the least bit revealing, and I mean the ones that fit. But he's gone now thanks to one particular sexy guy."

While I hid my body and my pretty underwear sets from Jason the Jerk beneath baggy clothes, Maverick got to see them. My underwear *and* my body. And he liked them. A lot.

Lindy was right way back when and she was right now.

I pulled out lavender lace panties and pulled them on beneath my towel.

"You know calling Maverick James sexy is being hypocritical. That's why Jason got fired."

"There's no similarity at all," she replied. "Because it's not a power thing. You called me because you *want* to tease your new boss with that hot little bod of yours."

I grabbed my glasses and frowned while I did it. I hated when she was right.

"You're wearing this green top with this skirt." It was the shirt I'd ordered online and a jean skirt and she wasn't asking, she was telling. "As for makeup, let me see what you've got."

She went into the bathroom and I got dressed.

"Don't think for one second I've forgotten that you got eaten out by Maverick James," she said from the bathroom.

I didn't think she would. I was impressed she held off this long to bring it up.

I pulled the shirt over my head, then smoothed it down. It had a V neckline and while it wasn't inappropriate, looking down I had a good view of my cleavage. What there was of it, at least.

She came out holding a lip gloss. "Didn't we get this for a seventh-grade dance?" She sniffed it. "It's cherry flavored. Okay, that's just wrong."

I bit my lip and nodded. She went to the trash can and dropped it in. "We'll raid Lindy's stash. Where is she, anyway?"

"Not sure. She wasn't here when I got back."

"So... Maverick's pussy snack. Did you sit on his face or were you at the edge of the bed or–"

"Mal!" I cried, my cheeks heating. "I'm not telling you that."

"Yes, you are."

"No, I'm not. We kissed last night," I began, giving her something.

"Last night?" Her perfectly arched eyebrows went

up. "You mean at the office? You kissed Jake Ryan after I walked out?"

I nodded, then bit back a smile. "It was *nothing* like the movie."

At the end of *Sixteen Candles,* Jake and Samantha kissed sweetly and innocently over a birthday cake. What Mav and I did was far from innocent or sweet.

"Late last night, he emailed me a sex quiz back," I told her, catching her up.

She frowned, then her eyes widened. "Holy shit. That didn't happen in the movie. I bet every word was hot."

I couldn't help but grin. "It was. God, yes. He did it so I have it as protection. So that I'm comfortable because he read mine. I can sue him or–"

"Get a shit ton of money out of the guy if you wanted. Wow." Mal's enthusiasm softened. "Bridge, I like this guy."

I licked my lips, dropped onto my bed. "I do, too."

"So he went downtown before you had sex."

I shook my head. "We didn't have sex. We were going to, but his brothers showed up."

"Including Theo."

I rolled my eyes. "God, yes. Including Theo."

"Is he nice?"

"Theo?"

"Yes, Theo."

"Quiet. He's a doctor. Trauma surgeon."

"Ooh, hot and a doctor." Mal fanned herself. "I wonder if *he's* hungry. I've got something for him to eat."

I popped up from the bed. "Oh my God. The way you talk, you'll get along great with Dex. He's the youngest and a professional hockey player."

"Two billionaire CEOs, a doctor and a pro hockey player?" She ticked them off with her fingers. "God, their parents must be proud."

I went to the mirror and fiddled with my hair. Up? Down?

"They said their father died, but they weren't the least bit upset by it. I guess he was an asshole. As for his mother, Mav mentioned–"

"Mav? It's Mav now? I guess if he's had his face between your thighs you can call him that."

"–that she's nice and interested in grandkids."

I remembered my parents, although through the memories of a ten-year-old. They'd been in love. Were happy. Fun. My dad was a teacher, my mom a florist. I remember carpool and swim lessons. Skiing and sledding.

I would never have a relationship with them as an adult and I wondered if I'd think of them differently, like Lindy probably did, since she'd been twenty-three when they died.

"Don't touch your hair," she ordered. "Leave it down and don't even think about putting it in a hair tie. I bet *Mav* will like it that way. So... back to his eating habits. He's not done with you."

I spun around to face her. She was hugging my rainbow pillow I'd gotten when I was twelve. "How do you know that?"

"You said you were interrupted by his brothers. Did he come?"

"No."

"That man is either a superhero or has the worst case of blue balls."

I hadn't seen his balls, but his dick had been all kinds of hard.

"He's not done with you." She glanced at her watch. "Let's get your makeup done. I can't wait to meet Theo."

"I think Dex is a better match," I told her, although two hard-core extroverts getting together could be a natural disaster.

"We're meeting him at the restaurant?"

I shrugged. "I guess so. We didn't decide when he dropped me off."

"Because you two were probably playing tonsil hockey at the door."

I didn't say anything because that was completely accurate.

27

MAVERICK

I KNOCKED on Bridget's front door to pick her up for dinner and waited. I'd been doing that for the past two hours since I dropped her off to shower and change clothes. I kissed her thoroughly but that hadn't been enough. After what we did on my couch... fuck, I was going crazy. Craving to be with her. Aching to be in her.

Dinner plans could go fuck themselves because as soon as Bridget opened her door, I'd push her inside and make her come all over my cock in all the ways I'd imagined. And even though it had been a short time since we met, I had lots of ways.

My brothers could amuse themselves without us. Hunter Valley had plenty to keep them entertained that didn't involve me or Bridget for the rest of the night. Or their time in the state.

But it wasn't Bridget that answered, but a pretty blonde.

"Hello," she said, her voice smooth and warm that matched her smile. I guessed her age to be close to mine. Mid-thirties. She wore a pretty green sundress, and her hair was pulled up and back somehow with wisps that artfully framed her face. Her makeup was light but expertly applied. She looked... perfect.

My mother would love her.

I took in the house again, confirming I didn't accidentally knock on the wrong one. My dick had been in charge earlier and it was driving me now.

"Hi. Um, I'm here for Bridget."

"She's not here. Can I help you?" she asked, her blue eyes raking over me as she considered all the ways she might be able to help. Like out of my pants. I couldn't miss her thorough review. Appreciatively and not subtly. It wasn't inappropriate, but the gaze of a woman who saw something she liked.

I might've been interested because she was pretty, age appropriate and had no ring on her finger. But that was before Bridget. It seemed my dick and I had a thing for petite, shy brunettes who came just for me.

"I'm Maverick James. Her..." I paused for a second because I wanted to say boyfriend, but I felt too old for that term. Besides, Bridget and I hadn't talked about a relationship–which we were in even if she didn't know it–for me to share it yet with anyone. "...boss."

Awareness lit the woman's eyes. "Oh, right. James Corp. I'm her sister, Lindy."

Bridget's sister, the one who had probably taken care of her after their parents died. Her much older, very blonde sister. Shit. She was the one I should be into. A woman who wasn't fifteen years younger.

I didn't need this woman to think I was a dirty old man, fingerfucking her little sister. Shit, I was one. But Bridget liked it. No, loved it. Coming for me and *only* me. She didn't care about my age. I had a feeling it got her hot, me being older. Being in charge and watching out for her. Because a twenty-two-year-old boy wasn't going to be able to do that for her. He wouldn't give her what she needed. The proof of it had been in her sex quiz.

I offered my hand and she shook it.

"Nice to meet you," she said. "I was out this afternoon so I don't know what she's doing. Would you like to come in and wait for her? I can get you some coffee, a drink perhaps?"

She just asked me in for a drink. Yeah, she was interested in me, and I admired her for her efforts, but I felt uncomfortable because of it. I'd had my head between her little sister's thighs only a few hours earlier.

"Thanks, but no. I think Bridget and I got our wires crossed."

I stepped back and Lindy looked disappointed.

"I'll tell her you stopped by," she said. "Maybe I'll see you again."

"You definitely will," I replied confidently. Only because Lindy was Bridget's sister and if I kept Bridget, I kept the sister. "Thanks."

Her eyes brightened and I realized she may have misunderstood. I wasn't going to fix it now and hopefully it would become clear to everyone–including Bridget–soon enough.

I went back to my car to figure out where the hell Bridget was. If she'd run again, I wouldn't spank her, because as we both learned, she'd like it too much. Maybe a plug in her ass. It would be awfully hard to run off with one of those nice and deep.

28

BRIDGET

WHEN MAV CAME into the restaurant, my first thought was, God, he was hot. The second was that he was angry.

I swallowed hard.

"I told you he wanted to pick you up," Dex leaned close and murmured as his brother weaved around the tables.

We were at a local brew pub that was popular for its outdoor seating, like Kincaids the night before. Since it was Saturday, the place was already full. Since the place was owned by Mal's brother, Arlo, she'd called ahead and he kept a prime table for us.

We had drinks in front of us but hadn't ordered any food.

Mallory's obsession with Theo was short-lived when he told her he was dating someone. Silas and Dex frowned–practically grimaced–when he shared that, so I had to assume they didn't like her. Her name was Maude and she was a podiatrist who worked at the same hospital. Mallory had taken it in her usual laid-back way and was enjoying Dex's stories, which he never seemed to be short of.

Mav stopped right in front of my chair, reached down and pulled me to my feet. He cupped my jaw, then kissed me. Like seriously kissed me, right in the middle of the patio.

Someone whistled.

Mav only lifted his head when he was good and finished with the kiss.

I was wobbly and hot all over. He'd given me two orgasms earlier while he'd had none. I thought of Mallory's comment about his blue balls and blamed his grumpy attitude on that.

"Baby, why didn't you wait for me?" he asked. With him leaning down, his dark eyes were right in front of mine. I couldn't see anyone else but him.

"I... I didn't know you were coming back."

"I'm sorry I didn't make things clear," he said. "But

know this. You're my girl, I pick you up."

"See?" Silas called, but I didn't look his way. Neither did Mav.

I blinked at him, surprised and confused. "I'm your girl?"

His jaw clenched and... yup, blue balls. Leaning in a little further, he put his mouth right by my ear so only I could hear his next words. "Whose pussy did I lick earlier?"

I flushed from the top of my head to the tips of my toes. "Mine," I whispered.

"Then you're my girl."

"But–"

"Do you want to be my good girl or bad girl tonight? Either way, you're getting fucked. Remember, I have a fantasy list."

My mouth dropped open and my pussy clenched, remembering what he'd done to me and that hadn't even touched his email list.

He wasn't fazed talking dirty right in the middle of a restaurant. With people all around. With his brothers, and Mallory, right there. He didn't care.

I wasn't a secret.

And that was the difference between him and my professor. Mav was... proud of me, proud of whatever *us* was and it had only been one day.

"I want to be your good girl," I admitted, a little scared and a little thrilled.

I'd jumped in with my professor and I'd gotten hurt. No, fucked over. Completely and totally fucked over. Jason Jimenez had been a weekday reminder of how men could be dicks.

Mav, though, he wasn't a dick. Or didn't seem to be. Mallory had pretty good radar when it came to assholes–unlike mine which seemed to be broken– and wasn't telling me to tell Mav to fuck off. No, she *wanted* me to fuck him. It seemed so did his brothers.

Mav's hand curled around and cupped my nape in a possessive hold. The corner of his mouth tipped up in a smile that was just for me. "That's right, baby."

"Some of us aren't getting any, so sit the fuck down."

That was Silas grumbling.

Mav settled in the chair I'd been in, then pulled me onto his lap.

"Mav!" I cried. "I can't sit here all night."

He leaned in again, kissed my temple. "Be a good girl and hide how hard I am from your friend and my brothers. Hell, the entire bar."

I wiggled my butt and felt him twitch, rock hard and ready beneath me.

Grabbing my drink, I took a big sip, needing to cool off, but didn't think that was going to cut it.

29

MAVERICK

"–SHE said that her mommy and daddy were wrestling upstairs in bed."

Mallory was sharing stories her first graders had told her, making me wonder how she kept a straight face when she ran into the parents around town. She'd just finished her first year as a teacher, having finished college a year early since she'd taken summer classes.

"Did you always want to teach?" Silas asked, listening to her closely.

Mallory nodded. "I did. Bridge and I used to play school when we were little. I, of course, was the teacher. It never went well because Bridge is too fucking smart and knew all the answers."

Bridget squirmed in my lap, which felt amazing, and like the worst kind of torture. While I'd been hard since I first saw her at the coffee shop, my dick had been throbbing since we were interrupted earlier. I wasn't kidding when I needed her to hide my hard on but feeling her perfect ass wiggle around wasn't helping.

I wanted to toss her over my shoulder and carry her out of here. Hopefully that would make enough of a scene that no one would pay any attention to the lead pipe I had down the inside of my leg. And maybe that caveman-like action would get the fact that Bridget was my girl through that smart head of hers.

It was as if the connection we'd shared earlier was forgotten. No, not forgotten. *Questioned.* Again.

Leaving her off at her house with only a kiss and no further direction or intention had been a mistake. I needed to tell her, straight out, what was going to happen next.

"Maybe she should be a teacher then instead of working for my dumbass brother."

"Hey, she works for me, too," Silas added.

Silas and I both left college and went right into the

family business. Even though I was CEO, he and I worked side by side, making all the important decisions together.

"That's what I said!" Mallory explained. "I've been wanting her to take the job teaching Physics at the high school."

All four of us grimaced, even Theo who'd had to take all kinds of science classes to be a doctor, at the idea of having to do high school Physics again, let alone teach it.

"I don't have a teaching license," Bridget reminded her.

Mallory waved that off. "You'll be a long-term sub and won't need one. Mrs. Birdsong is having her baby in September and plans to be out at least through January."

"The fact that the school district gets away with having someone teach kids for that long without any credentials is a little scary," Bridget muttered.

Mallory leaned in, resting on her forearms on the table. I only saw this woman being bold and brash, but her gaze on Bridget was serious. "The fact that you don't think you're qualified to teach the subject is a little scary. You have an eidetic memory and went to MIT for Christ's sake."

"You went to MIT?" Silas asked, whistling again. Impressed.

Bridget nodded.

"Engineering, math, computer sciences?" Theo asked.

"Pure math," she said.

I didn't even know what the hell that was. The blank look on everyone else's faces indicated they didn't either.

"What's your job with James Corp?" Dex asked.

"Assistant."

"You're interested in the hospitality industry?" he wondered, meaning everything to do with hotels.

Bridget shook her head. "There was an opening and I applied. I needed the job."

"With a degree from MIT, you can probably take a few online college classes to get the teacher's certificate," Theo said, returning back to the Physics class. "That is, if that's what you want to do."

Bridget squirmed some more and I set my hands on her hips to hold her still.

"I didn't graduate."

She was in profile since she was on my lap and saw the words cost her. Glancing at Mallory, I noticed she was far from her usual happy self. She was biting her lip and looked angry.

"How come?" Dex pushed. For once, I was glad he did because I wanted to know.

"There was an issue with a paper."

"Bullshit," Mallory said, making it into a cough.

"Mal!" Bridget said, her eyes imploring.

"Come on," Mallory said, dragging out the words. "Enough already. There wasn't an issue with a paper. Your professor, that Diego fucker, published your thesis work in an academic journal as his own and let the school kick you out for plagiarism."

I went still beneath her. My fingers clenched her hips though and I felt the ripple of... something move through her. Anger. Shame. Frustration.

I knew what I felt. Rage.

"Holy shit, that's a dick move," Dex said, running a hand through his hair.

A dick move? *A dick move!*

"Why didn't you report him?" Theo asked. "If you had the notes then you could prove–"

Bridget shook her head and tried to stand, but I kept her still because she wasn't running away. I had that part of her figured out. It was Mallory who cut him off.

"Because Professor Asshole seduced her and–"

Now it was my turn to interrupt because I knew

how she was going to finish. "–used his position of power to make her afraid."

Now it all made sense. Her hesitancy with me. Her running.

Holy fuck.

30

MAVERICK

DEX DRAGGED Mallory off to the hatchet tossing inside. I'd never been to a restaurant that had it before, but I took in the space when I cut through the restaurant. If there was anyone who wanted to throw sharp objects it was me.

Her professor had seduced Bridget to get her work. Used it as his own. Let her be expelled in what, her senior year, for plagiarism? I didn't know anything about the jobs or field of math, but I assumed it had to be a small group, especially at that elite level. Being labeled a plagiarist couldn't be good for her chance of ever finishing her degree, or a career.

So she'd run, proverbial tail between her legs, back to Hunter Valley and got a job at James Corp. Being an assistant on a construction project wasn't her dream job. Of course it wasn't. Especially working day after day for a dick like Jimenez.

I had to wonder if her dream had been destroyed by one careless, dickless fucker. The guy who was the 1 on her sex quiz. The only guy who she'd been with had used her.

I'd get her to tell me what her dream was, then help her achieve it. Because she'd been screwed over enough.

No one was going to fuck with her now.

Hell, the fuck, no.

Yeah, I wanted to throw some shit. Starting with a man in Massachusetts.

But I couldn't. I had to focus on Bridget. On the here and now.

Like right fucking now.

With my hands on her hips, I lifted Bridget to her feet, then stood. I took her hand, ensuring she didn't run, but also so she knew my next move included her.

"We're getting out of here."

Theo and Silas nodded, but didn't say anything, only gave me looks that told me without words that they were going to help finish that fucker.

He was going down.

Down.

"Come on, baby," I said, kissing her temple, then leading her out of the restaurant and to my car.

31

BRIDGET

Mav held the door for me, and I climbed into his car. Instead of shutting it, he squatted down.

"Are you okay?" he asked.

His eyes were level with mine and they roved over my face, drifting from them to my mouth and back.

"I'm fine." I wasn't lying. I was used to the feel of living with what my professor did. Mallory was still obviously pissed and now so were the James brothers.

He reached out and took my hand, ran his thumb–in a very distracting way–over my knuckles. "I want you to come home with me, because, well, I'm selfish and want you there so I know you're safe, but I'll take you home instead if you're not comfortable."

He needed to be reassured by me? That made no sense. Except, I'd had months to process it, Mav had had ten minutes.

"It was a while ago now. I'm over it."

He frowned. "No, you're not."

I sighed. "I'm not, but I'm moving on. I have no choice."

"Yes, you do. Fight him. Sue him. Prove he stole from you."

I shook my head. "It's his word against mine. A tenured professor versus a student?"

"You're so smart that–"

"Everyone there is smart. I'm not all that special."

His eyes narrowed. "What did I say about that kind of talk?"

I had to laugh. "All I'm saying is that it's like the Olympics. Compared to everyone else at home, you're an incredibly fast skier or runner. Then when you show up at the Olympics, *everyone* is as good as you. Or better. I'm not the only one good at math at MIT."

"Then you'd have won the Math Olympics gold medal because a tenured professor stole from *you.*"

He had a point.

"I don't have the money to sue him. Or whatever. It's done." I had the hottest pseudo-lumberjack in front of me. The last thing I wanted to talk, or think about, was Professor Diego.

The look Mav was giving me didn't indicate that it was done. At all.

"I want you to kiss me," I told him, my gaze latched onto his lips. "That's what I want."

I did. I wanted that really bad. We were interrupted earlier, and I wanted to know what Mav would have done if his brothers hadn't rang the doorbell. He'd given me orgasms and I was addicted. I hadn't known what I'd been missing, but I craved it now. Maybe I was sex starved after all.

A slow smile crept across his face and his dark eyes dropped to my lips. "That I can do."

His hand slid up my arm and cupped the back of my neck, tugged gently on my hair, making me gasp.

He kissed me then, not gently. Not sweetly. Hell, no. This was as if I was his source of oxygen and he was taking, taking, taking.

I moaned. He tipped my head, then growled, taking my lips again, then working along my jaw.

He tasted me. Licked. Sucked. Nipped.

"Mav," I whispered. We were in a little pocket of

quiet between cars in the parking lot. I felt sheltered and safe with him.

"I like this shirt," he murmured, his finger sliding back and forth along the neckline. "I'd like it on my floor even more."

"Okay," I whispered, liking that idea very much. Until earlier, I hadn't even known the level of pleasure Mav had given me. That it was even possible. He knew I hadn't come with or from a guy before and seemed to have made it his mission to get me off.

If I had to rate his job performance, he'd get a promotion and a raise and a corner office.

He stood and I had a quick view of the thick outline of his dick in his jeans before he closed my door, went around the car and settled into the driver's seat.

As he turned the car on, he looked at me. The stare was penetrating, filled with heat. Need. Intensity.

I swallowed and rubbed my thighs together.

He noticed and a growl escaped through gritted teeth.

Putting the car in gear, he looked over his shoulder and backed out of the parking lot.

If I was horny–which was an adjective I never used on myself before–and a little frantic for more than just the kiss, then Mav had to be ten times worse. Squared. Cubed.

I'd been naked in his lap. Sprawled on his bed. He'd had his big, ridiculously hard and amazing looking dick in hand. Then denied.

As he drove out of town, I set my hand on his thigh. The hard muscle clenched beneath my palm. I didn't linger there, but slid upward, higher and higher until I felt the swollen head and then the thick length. Cupping it, I gave it a squeeze.

The car veered slightly, but he recorrected.

"Baby," he said, his gaze torn from the road for a second to meet mine. "You can't do that while I'm driving."

I bit my lip, felt brave. Stroked him again, then undid the button on his jeans and slid down the zipper to reach inside.

"Jesus. Fuck." His hips bucked when I touched him directly for the first time. Hot, silky flesh over steel.

Jesus. Fuck, I thought. I had no idea a dick went down a pant leg. I saw underwear models in magazine ads and they didn't do that. Obviously. And yes, I looked.

Mav was bigger than any of those models. Longer. Thicker. At least what I saw of it earlier and what I felt now.

"Baby," he said again, and I swore he got bigger in my hold.

My pussy clenched and I wondered if he'd fit inside me because he was big. B.I.G.

"Do you want me to stop?" I asked, watching as his knuckles turned white as he gripped the wheel.

I definitely didn't, but I didn't want to be found in a ditch with my hand down his pants by firefighters.

He moved a hand down to rest over mine inside the front of his jeans. Pressed down. Moved my hand how he liked.

"Fuck," he growled again after a minute, then yanked my hand away and set it on my own thigh. He held it hostage there. "I'm not coming in my boxers. I'm coming in that hot little pussy, so be a good girl and don't tempt me."

"Mav," I began, but he stopped me.

"Shh. No talking, no more squirming like that. I see you squeezing those thighs together."

I knew the way to his place now and we took the last few turns practically on two wheels.

When he turned off the car out front, he didn't linger. Came around and helped me out. He hadn't even adjusted his jeans. The front was open and his boxers pushed down exposing him, so big and hard. It was a good thing he had no neighbors, not just because of his dick, but because he turned and pushed me up against the car.

"You've been a bad girl, baby." His voice was a husky whisper.

32

MAVERICK

I MEANT WHAT I SAID. She was so fucking bad sticking her hand in my pants as I was driving. I almost put us in a ditch twice. It was when she gripped me at the base and couldn't wrap her fingers all the way around me that I thought I was going to come. I'd had this exact fantasy in the shower the night before. I was ready to pull her hand free, but I'd showed her how to stroke me so good instead.

Then I nearly came. I was thirty-seven years old and almost blew like a teenager with zero control.

And that made Bridget so fucking bad.

She lifted her gaze and I saw the want in her green

eyes. She didn't know her full power yet, the fact that I could see the upper swells of her perfect little tits with each pant of breath. That her cheeks were flushed and her hands were sliding over my chest without her even realizing.

This woman could bring me to my knees. She almost had and I needed to take a little fucking control back. I took a breath, then another, thought about baseball stats and any other boring thing to bring myself from spinning her around so she faced the hood of the car, bending her over it and ramming my dick home so she cried out loud enough even the neighbor way down the road would know I took my girl nice and deep.

I growled again, because that had *not* helped.

Taking her hand, I tugged her to the door, pushed in the lock code and got us inside.

"Strip," I told her as I kicked the door shut.

I set my hands on my hips as she pushed her glasses up. Licked her lips. Thought.

That wouldn't do. She wanted me to shut her thoughts down and that was what I was going to do.

"Now, baby."

She grabbed the hem of her shirt and pulled it off over her head. Her hair slid side to side as it settled back over her shoulders.

"Wait," I told her, holding up a hand as she reached behind her back.

Fuck. She had on a pale purple bra that only covered the lower half of her tits. A hint of the upper curve of her nipples peeked out.

"The bottoms match?"

Looking up through her lashes, she nodded.

"Show me."

After she toed off her sandals, she rid herself of her skirt.

"So fucking perfect," I murmured, looking into her eyes so she knew I meant it. Then I couldn't resist, raking my gaze down her. Pert tits, purple lace covered pussy, toned legs. "On your knees."

I held out a hand and she took it to settle before me. There was a rug in the entryway so the floor would be soft beneath her.

With my jeans open, it was easy to push them, along with my boxers, down enough so my dick was completely free. Fuck that felt good, but I knew what would feel better.

"You wanted my dick in the car. It's all yours, baby."

I stepped close and gripped the base. She didn't have to move much, just rise up onto her knees fully and lean forward a few inches to lick me like a fucking ice cream cone.

"Shit."

Then she took the head into her mouth and my knees almost buckled. I locked them out and cupped the back of her head, careful not to ram my dick down her throat like I wanted.

"Look at you, baby, fitting my dick in that hot little mouth."

With one hand braced on my thigh, she sucked, hollowing her cheeks.

"That's right. Make me feel good for how you treated me in the car."

She took more of me, but there was no way she could swallow me down. I was too big. It was hot enough watching her attempt it, knowing she'd try and try and never get it all.

My balls drew up with her enthusiasm and eagerness to please.

As she wetly sucked, her hips began to squirm and her free hand moved down between her legs, slipping beneath her panties.

I pulled my hips back and her lips slipped off of me. I tugged on her hair so her gaze lifted to mine.

"Who makes you come, baby?"

"You," she whispered, licking her slick, swollen lips.

"That's right. Is that pussy all wet for me?"

She nodded.

"Show me."

Her hand slipped from her panties and she lifted it up, two fingers raised. They were sticky and slick. Holding her wrist, I leaned down and sucked them clean.

"Good girl getting all wet from sucking my dick."

I was in charge of her and it got her off. She wanted someone else to be in a position of power over her, but in the right way. All she'd had was shit men.

That stopped now.

Probably in that smart brain of hers, she knew she was the one guiding us. That while she was on her knees, she had all the fucking power. My dick was hard because she was aroused by the idea of an *us*. It was so complicated, yet so simple at the same time.

I might be over a hundred pounds bigger, but Bridget would *always* be in control because she had me by the fucking balls. If she wanted something, I'd give it to her. If she got wet from it, it was a guarantee I'd be hard.

The more she gave me, the more *I* was the one crawling to her.

"You ready to get fucked, baby?"

"Please, Mav." Her voice was a soft whisper, almost a beg.

"Since you asked so nicely."

Carefully, I took off her glasses, then reached down and tossed her over my shoulder, carrying her to the master bedroom.

33

BRIDGET

IT SEEMED Mav liked to carry me around like a caveman.

I was okay with that.

Really, okay.

Slowly, he lowered me down his body and it only reminded me how big and strong he was.

With deft fingers, he reached behind me and unclasped my bra and it fell to my feet.

"I want to see you too," I said.

He took a step back, eyed me with open amusement and keen desire. "You want to see me?"

I nodded.

Reaching behind his neck, he tugged off his t-shirt in the sexy way that defied logic. Inch by inch, his chest was revealed. All tanned, toned perfection. And acres of it.

With his jeans around his hips, they slouched and if his dick wasn't curved up and bobbing by his navel, he'd look like one of those calendar models.

I swirled my finger in the air indicating the pants had to come off and he arched a brow. A smirk curled the corner of his mouth as he pushed them down, and worked them along with his shoes, off.

"Wow," I said, taking a step back and dropping onto the edge of the bed. He was an incredible specimen of a man. Bigger. Bulkier. More muscles. More... everything.

"With that mouth hanging open like that, it makes me think you want me to fill it again," he said as he went over to the bedside table and grabbed the brand-new box of condoms I hadn't noticed. He ripped it open and grabbed a strip, dropping it on the bed.

I snapped my mouth closed. Not because I didn't want to watch how he lost control as I sucked and licked him, but because my pussy throbbed. Ached.

"You teased me earlier," I reminded, staring at the condoms. There were at least five connected together and briefly wondered if he planned on using all of them tonight.

A dark brow went up and he prowled closer. Yes, that look indicated he did plan to use all of them.

With a hand on the center of my chest, he gave me a gentle push and I fell back on the bed. He hooked a finger in my panties and slid them down my legs.

"You were the one who came twice," he reminded. "How is that teasing?"

With a hand at my hip, he shifted me so I was in the middle of the bed. Putting one knee up, he crawled over me. Loomed.

I glanced at his chest, set my palm there.

"Baby. You had my dick in your mouth. Don't go all shy on me now." With his big hand, he pushed my hair back from my face. "How is that teasing?" he asked again. His woodsy scent was heady. So was the heat from his body, the way he was settled between my thighs.

"You said I was your good girl but didn't give me your dick."

His dark eyes flared and his jaw clenched. He pushed back so he sat back on his heels and grabbed the strip of condoms and ripped one off. With his teeth, he opened the wrapper and I watched as he rolled it down his length.

Then he set a hand by my head again and let the other roam, cupping my breasts, pinching my nipples, then sliding down and cupping me.

"So wet. All for me?"

I nodded, then he slipped one thick finger inside and my eyes fell closed. He worked me with it until I was writhing beneath him, then he added a second.

My back arched and I pulled my knees up because he wasn't touching my clit like I wanted.

"Mav!" I cried.

"Gotta make sure you're ready. This little pussy needs to be all wet and greedy to take all of me."

"It's ready," I said, grabbing his wrist. "It's *so* ready."

He pulled his fingers away, then gripped himself, sliding the blunt head through my folds. It bumped my clit and I got closer to coming. Now that I knew what Mav could do, I was frantic and needy for it.

Settling at my entrance, he dropped to his forearm, holding his weight off me but now our chests touched. His hand cupped my face and gripped my hair.

"Look at me."

I did.

He pushed in, one very fat inch at a time.

Holy. Shit.

34

MAVERICK

HOLY FUCK, she was tight. Her pussy was snug and with every inch I gave her, she wiggled and squirmed as she stretched open.

She began to pant and every time her chest rose, her hard nipples brushed against me.

I thought her mouth was perfect. This?

Fuck.

I gritted my teeth and carefully worked my way into her, pulling back, pushing deeper. And deeper.

She whimpered, clenched her inner walls. Just as I'd thought, I was a little too big and she had a difficult time taking me.

"Mav," she whispered.

Her eyes were wide with every inch I filled her.

"Shh, baby. Fuck, you feel so good. That little pussy's taking me so well. Remember, good girls get every inch of my dick. You can do it. That's it. Oh, you took a little more."

My girl loved dirty talk. It made her hot. And really fucking wet. To get in her, I had to take my time which was the sweetest torture. But I'd get in her and then I'd fuck her, mold her to my dick.

Leaning on one arm, I licked my thumb then worked it between us, circling over her swollen clit to soften her up even more.

"Mav!" she cried at the additional sensation and I sank in almost all the way.

"That's it. My baby's taking me so good. Open those legs even wider." She did, as far as she could. I thrust hard and finished the task.

Her fingers clawed into my sides as she rippled around me. I kept working her clit as I slowly pulled back, then filled her again. It was so fucking good, I wasn't going to make it.

In. Out. A little harder. A little faster now that she fit all of me.

My girl would always come first so I watched her closely. Felt her. The dig of her nails. The clench of her pussy. The sweet release of her arousal all over my dick. The throb of her clit.

"Come for me, baby. Come all over me."

My voice was rough because I was trying to catch my breath.

"Mav, I–oh... yes. Yes. YES!"

She came so hard I would swear her pussy was strangling my dick. I grabbed an ankle, raised it to my chest, then hooked the other and did the same, her young body so flexible. In this position, I could see my dick disappearing in her, then pulling out all covered in all her cream. Her pussy lips were stretched wide around me and I was angry to have the condom separating us.

My balls drew up and I felt the release at the base of my dick. I wanted to come inside her, coat her in my seed. Mark her inside and out. Fuck, make her mine in all ways.

I was a bastard for wanting this, but I couldn't help it. I fucked in the past for release, to empty my balls, but not for this connection. It had never been like this, and I expected it never would be again. Squeezing her ankles, I leaned forward, bending her almost in half as I thrust deep and held still. Burying the head of my dick so far in her she'd feel it for a few days.

I came on a rough growl, filling the condom with spurt after thick spurt of my release.

"Look what you did, making me come so hard. All for you, baby," I said when only little pulses of cum came from me. Lowering her legs, I settled over her. Kissed her. Our sweaty skin clung. Our breaths mingled. "You'll take only my big dick from now on."

She nodded and I pulled back enough to kiss her forehead, then look down in her sated, sleepy eyes.

I pulled out and took care of the condom. When I came back from the bathroom, I lifted her, pulled back the bedding so it was slung over the footboard, then settled her into the bed once again. I slid in beside her, pushed her hair back again.

"You sore?"

I couldn't miss the hot flush to her cheeks and the way it spread down her chest. Even after what we just did, she was shy.

"A little," she admitted.

I moved lower, nudged her knees wide and settled between them again.

"Mav, what–"

"Don't worry, I'll make it better," I said, right before I kissed her hot, swollen pussy. Licked it and gently brought her to not one, but two more orgasms.

She was a sweaty, whimpering mess when I wiped

my mouth with the back of my hand, then settled onto my back. She was so small, I pulled her on top of me, my hard dick nestled between her thighs. She wouldn't need a blanket with my heat.

"Mav," she said finally.

"Hmm?" Absently, I ran a hand up and down her back.

"Why me? Why now? I mean, you're older and–"

"You saying I'm too old for you, baby?" I asked.

She shook her head against my chest. "No, but you're... you. Why haven't you been taken?" she wondered.

I stilled, stared up at the coffered ceiling.

"I think I was waiting for you." I didn't know why I said that, but... it was true.

Maybe I had been living my life until it was time to find Bridget Beckett.

35

BRIDGET

"WHERE WERE YOU?" Lindy asked, coming out of the kitchen.

I hadn't even shut the door behind me before she asked.

She moved to the front window, saw Mav drive off.

"Is that... is that your boss?" she asked, eyes wide.

I felt like I was floating on a cloud of happiness and Lindy was ruining it.

Oh my God. Last night. And this morning. My pussy ached and I was beyond happy and sated and... yeah.

"Maverick James. Yes."

Her judging gaze raked over me. "Oh my God. You spent the night with him."

I was sure I looked like I was thoroughly ravaged, my hair a mess and I was sure he'd left another hickey on me somewhere she could see.

"He's your boss!"

"Don't make me feel bad about this, Lind," I said, shutting the door. I'd let go of my insecurities, my fear of being with a guy. I'd let go. Let my mind go blank and just... be. Mav knew what I needed and magically–and skillfully–gave it to me.

"You can't be serious. Do you know how old he is?" She asked, waving her arms. With her wet hair and robe, she must've just gotten out of the shower.

"Yes."

"You're twenty-two years old."

She was scolding me like I was sixteen and snuck out to go to a party.

I tipped up my chin. "I know how I old I am."

"He's... God, he's my age!"

I stilled and realized something. "How did you know he was my boss?" I asked.

She swallowed, but still glared at me. "He came to the house last night looking for you."

When he came to pick me up to take me to dinner. Of course she'd met him.

"Why did you have to pick the only eligible bachelor in town?" she yelled.

I processed her words and couldn't believe her reaction. "Oh my God. You're mad at me because I *stole* a thirty-something man from you?"

"Have you seen him?" She fanned herself.

"Of course I've seen him, I slept with him," I shouted back.

"Older men only want women your age for one thing," she countered. Her words stung and they were meant to. They made me feel silly and stupid.

"You don't have to remind me of that. My professor–" I bit my tongue, the truth falling out by mistake. "Mav's different."

She set her hands on her hips, cocked her head. "What about your professor?"

I turned away, set my purse on the table beside the door. I didn't want to get into this with her now. Or ever. Especially since she was mad. Irrationally so, but mad nonetheless.

"Bridge, what about your professor?" she pushed.

I wasn't going to get out of answering. Shit.

I closed my eyes, sighed. "He... he wanted my work, so he took it."

"What do you mean, took it?" she asked, her voice missing that angry edge.

"Took it," I repeated. "Claimed it as his."

She sighed, as if she were a balloon being deflated. "*That's* why you left?"

I cut past her, went into the kitchen hoping there was a pot of coffee. I couldn't look her in the eye when I told her this. "I didn't leave. I got kicked out because they said I plagiarized."

"Plagiarized what?" she asked, following.

I grabbed a mug from the cabinet and poured myself a cup. Took a big sip and burned my tongue.

"My professor's journal article."

"Oh my God! Are you fucking kidding me?" Now she was *really* mad.

"I know. I'm not perfect." I set my coffee down.

"That's what you think I'm upset about?" she shouted. "Jesus, Bridge. I'm your sister."

I shook my head and stared down at the counter.

"No. You're my mother and I can't ever live up to your expectations. I didn't mean to get expelled from MIT. Do you think I *wanted* to miss graduating and... and..." I didn't finish because there were so many *ands*.

I heard her drop into one of the kitchen chairs.

"Based on what you said, you slept with him, didn't you?" Her words were back to gentle.

I nodded.

"Oh, Bridge. He used you."

I spun around, pushed my glasses up. Now it was my turn to be angry, especially since she pointed out the most obvious thing ever. "I know! I know what he did! He stole from me. Took my work. Took my confidence. Ruined my chances at a career in Math. He stole *everything!*"

I started to cry, because, well, it sucked.

She came over and wrapped her arms around me.

"I'm sorry," she murmured, stroking my back. "God, I'm so sorry you think you can't share something like this with me. You let me think you dropped out and I didn't understand why you'd throw it all away. I must have hurt you with what I said, that you gave up and fuck, what else did I say to you?"

"That I was throwing my life away. That I'm so smart but am wasting it."

She pushed me back, set her hands on my shoulders. "I'm mad at you, Bridget Beckett. You made me be the bad guy here. You could have told me."

I shook my head. "I fell for the wrong guy and paid the price. I can't be perfect like you."

She laughed. "I am so far from perfect."

"Says the woman who lines her nail polish colors up by hue."

"Says the human calculator," she countered.

I had to laugh. It was that or cry.

"So. Maverick James."

It was my turn to sigh.

"I like him, Lindy. He's... God, he's amazing."

"I don't want to hear about his magical dick."

"I'm talking about *him*. He's nice. Sweet, if you can believe that. Ridiculously protective. He likes that I'm a nerd. And he has a magical dick."

She poked me in the side and stormed off. "I hate you!" she called, going upstairs.

"I hate you, too," I countered, smiling.

Happy.

36

MAVERICK

"Finally," Farrah said, when I answered her call. "I wasn't sure if you were dead. The only reason I knew you weren't is because Bradley told me."

I'd just gotten back from dropping Bridget off at her house. I wanted to keep her all day, but that wasn't possible. I had work to do. Non-Hunter Valley tasks that had to get done. A call with Japan and other meetings that Bradley had pushed off on Friday.

I pushed the button on the coffee maker and waited for it to brew.

"I'm alive. Busy. What's up?" I asked.

"I'm getting married."

I blinked. Watched the dark brew drip into the pot. "Excuse me?"

"Elise asked me to marry her."

Elise was her girlfriend of two years. Her *secret* girlfriend. While they'd been privately together, I'd gone with Farrah to dinners and events that required a date. Even my mother thought and hoped there could be something between us.

"We're getting married," she added. "On Saturday."

"Saturday? As in six days from now?" I asked. "That's fast."

"Yes." Farrah was a lawyer. Direct and to the point. She paused for a moment, took a deep breath. "I've been trying to get in touch with you. There's a problem."

"Okay."

"I assume you haven't been online." Now she sounded nervous.

"No. Where should I look?"

She gave the name of a local Denver social site that provided more gossip than fact. It didn't cover the news as much as people. Page Six type articles crossed with shady tabloids.

"I don't follow that shit." I didn't even want to check it out. I didn't follow rumor and speculation.

"Well, you should. We're in it. A photographer saw

my ring and assumed I'm engaged. That's true and all, but he also made the assumption that the groom is you."

"What?" I ran my hand through my hair, the hair that was all tousled from Bridget's fingers. "Are you fucking kidding me?"

"No. I first called to let you know Elise proposed. Then I called you to tell you we set the wedding date as soon as possible. You know, so my father won't have much time to fuck with me."

Her father and mine had been best friends. Assholes together for decades. We also had that in common, dicks for dads. Except mine didn't bother me any longer, thank fuck.

"But then things blew up."

I'd known Farrah all my life. We'd been friends growing up, and I'd been her confidant when she told me she was gay the winter break of our freshman year in college. Her family wouldn't be accepting or understanding of her sexuality and so she'd kept it a secret.

I'd kept it a secret for her. With her.

"Surprise," she said, not sounding the least bit excited. "We're getting married."

No wonder my mother had left four voicemails since last night.

To the world, I was engaged and about to wed. It was a fucking nightmare.

37

BRIDGET

THE FRONT DOOR OPENED, then slammed shut with enough force for the dishes to rattle in the cabinets.

"Bridge!" Mallory yelled. "BRIDGE!"

I ran out of the kitchen, Lindy hot on my heels. Ever since our little heart-to-heart earlier, things were better between us. Not in any tangible way, but it was... lighter. I didn't feel like I had to prove myself to her now.

Mallory's breaths were ragged as if she sprinted from her house. Eyes wide, she looked panicked. Wild.

"What?" I asked, a little panicked. I didn't remember Mal like this before. "What happened?"

"He's getting married," she said.

I glanced at Lindy, who shrugged.

"Who?" I asked.

"Maverick."

I frowned. He dropped me off two hours earlier. My pussy was still sore from what we did the night before.

"Your Maverick?" Lindy asked.

"How many Maverick's are there?" Mallory countered, then frowned, considering. "Besides the *Top Gun* movie, I don't know of any."

I hadn't seen Mallory this freaked since we went prom dress shopping and the one she'd been eyeing for weeks had been sold out in her size.

She crossed the room to me and pressed her cell into my hand. "Remember I did a search for him on Friday when you told me about him?"

I nodded, staring at the article on her phone, trying to process what I was reading.

"I set up an alert and I just got this." She pointed to the screen.

The title read *Denver Socialite Bags A Billionaire.* Beneath it was a photo of Maverick with an exotically beautiful woman. They were dressed for a black-tie event and she looked insanely good, like a Miss Universe pageant contestant in the evening wear competition. All she was missing was a sash. I had to admit they looked good together, how his hand rested on her waist in a possessive way. Perfect. I wasn't going to linger on how amazing Mav looked in a tuxedo. It had to be custom to have one in his size and fit so well.

Below the photo was a caption. *Farrah Cohen with her fiancé CEO Maverick James at the Children's Hospital Fundraiser in May.*

I skimmed the article.

Farrah Cohen was seen out and about in Denver yesterday with a five-carat diamond ring gracing her left hand. Word on the street is that her longtime boyfriend, Maverick James, popped the question. Miss Cohen confirmed that the wedding is to take place this weekend. This reporter is thrilled to report this match-made-in-heaven love story, but has to wonder as to the haste of the nuptials. Is there a Baby James on the way? Only time will tell. Photos and details of the wedding to come next week!

Oh. My. God. Farrah. He'd mentioned that name with his brothers.

I let my hand fall to my side. I stared at Mallory, but not seeing her. I saw Maverick kissing me goodbye this morning. Saw him hovering over me as he filled me for the first time last night. When he flipped me over and told me that while I was his good girl, he was going to fuck me like I was very, very bad.

"He's getting married," Mallory repeated, for no apparent reason.

"Married?" Lindy questioned in her *what the fuck* mom tone, snagging the cell.

"Married," I replied, completely numb.

"Jesus, this is just like in *Sixteen Candles,*" Mallory said. "I'm never doing anything movie related ever again."

Mav was getting married. To a gorgeous woman named Farrah.

Who he'd been dating for months and may have impregnated.

"He's getting married," Lindy finally said.

We stood in the living room, all of us silent.

"I was with him last night! This morning. He didn't say a word."

"He walked in the pooch parade," Mallory added, as if that was the clincher.

I ran into the kitchen and grabbed my cell, called him.

It rang and rang, then went to voicemail. I didn't leave one, because what could I say?

Mallory and Lindy stood in the doorway, watching.

I tried again. Voicemail. "Mav, I–" This time, that was all I got out, then hung up. Still lost.

Then I swiped into my work email, found one

from Bradley, Mav's assistant and grabbed his number from his signature footer. He answered before it rang twice.

"Bradley, this is Bridget Beckett on the Hunter Valley project." I fiddled with a Montana state magnet on the fridge as I spoke.

"Hello, Bridget." He was calm and confident for a Sunday.

"Um... I'm trying to get in touch with Mav–Maverick and he's not answering his phone."

"He's on a flight back to Denver right now. I'm sure he'll be in touch."

The Chinese menu the magnet held fell to the floor.

"He left?" I asked, my voice weaker than I wanted it to be.

Maverick had dropped me off after having sex with me, then left. Not just me, but the state.

"Yes. This morning. He has personal tasks to see to."

I had to admit, Bradley was the perfect assistant. Ever the diplomat.

"You mean to get married," I told him.

"Yes."

I looked to Mal and Lindy. "He's getting married."

If Bradley said it was happening, it was happening.

"Tell Mav..." My lip started to quiver, and I swallowed hard. "Tell him I... tell him to fuck off." Saying that, it was like the damn burst on my hurt. "That I trusted him. That he's the biggest fucking dick, and I know a number of them. I'm sure you got all that word for word. Don't worry about going to HR with it because I quit."

I hung up blindly since tears filled my eyes and I couldn't see.

I started to cry. Serious, hard-core crying.

"I'm... I... how could I be so stupid. Again?"

Arms circled me, pulled me in for a hug as I sobbed.

I'd let Maverick James in. Trusted him. Believed his words. That I was his good girl. That I was what he wanted. Needed. That he liked me just the way I was. That all he wanted from me was... me.

Yeah, right. All he wanted from me was to get laid. Used and left. Like usual. For being so smart, I was really fucking dumb.

38

MAVERICK

I WAITED for the flight attendant to open the private jet's entry door, Scout at my heels. I gave a curt smile to the woman and descended the steps.

It was hotter in Denver, especially on the tarmac. Brighter. I didn't want to be here. I wanted to be in Hunter Valley, with Bridget. In bed. In my shower. Hell, in the group of fucking Ponderosa pines.

I cut through the small terminal in a rush, Scout following, ready to deal with the shit that was going on. I'd had my head between Bridget's thighs at dawn, waking her up to me licking her clit and fingerfucking her to orgasm. Now, only a few hours later, I was in

Colorado and dealing with a not-so-secret fake fiancée. I knew this might come up someday. Hoped for it, in fact. Farrah deserved to fall in love and get married.

But why now? Why this fucking week when I just met Bridget? Things were good–no, fucking great–but shit, she had a history with asshole men who used her and left her. Treated her like shit. Stole from her. Hurt her heart.

Now she'd think it included me. Once she read about the wedding, she'd assume the worst. That I was no better than the guys who'd fucked her over before. No, worse. Because I knew what had happened with them, what she'd been through. I'd blatantly told her I wasn't like them, that she was *safe* with me. I'd literally asked her to trust me with her body *and* her heart.

She had and it had been so fucking amazing.

No doubt she thought I used her. Lied.

Fuck. *Fuck!*

Ever since I got to Montana, I'd ignored Farrah's calls. She was a friend and important to me, but I had more important things going on. Like being with Bridget.

I stalked across the parking lot to my car where I'd left it on Friday. Thinking too fucking hard as I did so.

I had to be in Denver to keep up the ruse. I'd been

her stand in for so long, I couldn't ruin it for her now. On the flight, I'd pulled up the first voicemail she'd left, told me to call her. The second said she needed to talk to me, that she had news. The next that her girlfriend, Elise, had proposed, and she'd accepted. That they were getting married.

Each message had ended with *Call me,* but I hadn't.

All of it had been a recap of her phone call.

After I hung up, Bradley had called. Said that the situation with Farrah was something I had to handle in Denver. Immediately. He told me about the same online article that Farrah had mentioned. I'd pulled it up while talking with him. It showed Farrah wearing a huge diamond ring. An engagement ring.

Fuck!

Then another article he directed me to that confirmed she was getting married. There was no outright mention that I was the groom, but since we'd been supposedly dating for months, I was the top choice.

Our ruse had worked. No one, social media or her family, suspected she was gay. All we'd done was attend events together, posed side by side in photos. I never slept with her. Hell, I never kissed her. She was the sister I never had and that was it. There was never news to share because we weren't really a couple.

Everyone had assumed we were hush hush about our private lives, which we were. But because of it, the press had filled in the blanks any way they wished.

I clicked the button on the key fob and unlocked the door, let Scout jump in and onto the passenger seat, then I climbed in. The windows slid down as soon as I started the engine and Scout stood on the door's armrest and stuck his head out.

My cell rang. Silas. "Where the fuck are you?" he snapped.

"Denver."

"It's true then."

I ran a hand over my face. "That I'm getting married? No."

"Right. Bradley called me. It's everywhere," he said. "Mav, I mean fucking *everywhere*."

I closed my eyes, slammed my hand down on the steering wheel. "Fuck."

"Were you going to tell me that you're getting married? I mean *Farrah*?"

"I'm... not... getting... married."

"Tell that to Farrah."

"She knows."

"Really? Because it sure as shit doesn't seem that way. Explain it to me. Explain the engagement ring that can be seen from space and your name tied to it."

I closed my eyes. Sighed. "I can't."

"What the fuck do you mean *you can't?*" he shouted.

"I can't," I said again. So fucking stuck. "It's not my story to tell."

It wasn't. I'd promised to keep Farrah's sexual orientation a secret. Her family was loaded and homophobic. While she wasn't a money grubber, her father's ridiculous rule about her inheritance being tied to her marriage was archaic and ridiculous. But all it stated was that for her to receive the money, she had to be legally wed. In the state of Colorado, that included same sex marriage. Farrah could marry the person she loved *and* get the family money she deserved.

While she'd been carefully–and secretly dating women, I'd played the role of boyfriend on the occasions when she needed a date. It hadn't been an issue. Until now. I hadn't dated anyone seriously in years, if really at all if I thought about it. It didn't matter to me if people thought Farrah and I were together. It was how I could be a friend to her.

Until. Fucking. Now.

The news of *who* she was marrying had to stay secret until the wedding, until there was no chance for her father to change any legal paperwork. It probably would have remained a secret except for her ring and some very snoopy paparazzi.

I couldn't deny any of it. I had to play along.

Silas was quiet for a second. "Jesus, Mav. What about Bridget? Did you at least explain it to her? Because she didn't seem to know you were engaged when she was screaming your name this morning."

At this point, I didn't care that he'd overheard us. Or that Dex and Theo probably had as well. I was cocky as hell that I was the man to bring Bridget pleasure. But I did care that he was right. When her pussy walls milked my fingers, I hadn't even known about the shitshow either.

"Fuck!"

"Yeah, fuck. After what we learned about her last night? About that douche nozzle professor? I don't think she's going to handle the news well."

That was an understatement of epic proportions. It was going to crush her and everything we'd been building together.

"I'll call her," I said. "Tell her."

"Tell her what, if you can't even tell me."

"I'll tell her to wait. To trust me."

Silas laughed. "Yeah, right. That woman's going to trust you? The guy who fucked her and fled. Who's all over the tabloids and social media as getting married to another woman in a few days? Who got her to trust her and then fucked her six ways to Sunday and then walked away? You have to be fucking blind not see she's fallen for you. She couldn't be any more used than a dirty dish at a Vegas buffet."

I groaned, then swore because his words hit me hard. And too accurate.

"I'll make this right. I have to. I... I've fallen for her."

"That is really fucking obvious. But a guy who's fallen for a woman isn't marrying someone else."

39

BRIDGET

MAVERICK CALLED. Texted. Multiple times. Thirty-seven, to be exact, before I blocked his number. I didn't want to hear what he had to say. Any of it. The lies. The excuses. The *Sorry, baby, but you were fun for the weekend. Be a good girl and fuck off now.*

I gave my phone to Lindy so I didn't search the internet for him. My laptop, too. I cried through the rest of Sunday. Monday, I didn't go to work. What was the point? I hadn't showered and didn't plan to. I hadn't slept. I wasn't going to be productive and the only thing I was needed for was to be a human calculator.

"Go to HR with Maverick's sex quiz. File a complaint. Sue," Lindy had advised, in one of her angry, spiteful moments. She brought me a cup of coffee in bed and I pulled the blanket back at the dark aroma. She and Mallory had been following the gossip columns for any change in the information, that Mav had gone to them and told them it was all wrong. That he wasn't marrying a Denver socialite on Saturday.

But he hadn't. And that meant I didn't want anything to do with him.

I was angry too, alternating between fits of crying and stomping around the house in bouts of rage. Then I'd climb back in bed and throw my covers over my head.

I shook my head, laying on my side, not interested in the coffee or anything else. "I'd have to talk to people about him. Tell them how much of a dupe I was. They'd no doubt look me up and see I have a track record of being a dumbass. Not only that, I'd probably be pulled into meetings or legal things with him present. I don't want to face him. I don't want to look at him. Hear his voice. I... I can't."

I pulled the pillow over my head and started to cry. Through my tears, I heard Lindy shut the door.

40

MAVERICK

"You're a dick," Dex said when I answered the phone.

I ran a hand over my face because I'd been hearing that a lot from my brothers. From Silas since he'd called me Sunday morning. From Theo before he'd come back to town and gone back to his sixteen-hour days at the hospital.

I was exhausted. Unshaven. If not for Scout needing to go outside, I wouldn't have left the house. I ran a billion-dollar company and I'd been reduced to day drinking on my couch with a dog for company.

Bradley had been running things for me. Who was

I kidding thinking that I accomplished anything with him as my assistant. These past few days proved that. And the fact that Silas had stepped in at the site meant I could be a sorry excuse for a human.

Now I was hearing it from Dex. "Besides what you've done to Bridget," he pushed on, "but I didn't even get an invitation to the wedding. I'm going to hang with Silas here in Hunter Valley since it's a cool as fuck town and he's doing *your* job."

I didn't miss the multiple low blows. They just kept on coming.

"I'm not getting married," I told him, gritting my teeth.

"That's what Silas told me, but I'm not sure how that works if every tabloid in the country says you are."

The wedding was tonight, thank fuck. I couldn't wait much longer to make things right with Bridget. Although I wasn't even sure after she learned the truth that she'd take me back. Because, like Dex said, I was a dick.

I felt like shit. I needed to tell someone because I was going out of my fucking mind because the *only* person I wanted to know what was happening wouldn't listen to me

My mother had called a million times, thrilled out

of her head. That only made me feel even more like shit. I couldn't tell her I wasn't the groom because she'd blab it to the world, but all I was concerned about–and Farrah, too–was the truth getting back to her father. The asshole.

"Because Farrah's marrying someone else," I told him.

"What? Then why doesn't she announce that? Why are you fucking moping around down there when you could be banging your young girlfriend? You're old and running out of time to keep getting it up."

"Fuck, Dex," I muttered. I had zero problem in that department with Bridget. I had a problem keeping it *down*.

"Who's the guy?" he asked.

"Elise," I muttered, rubbing my temple.

There, I fucking said it. Told Farrah's secret.

"The guy's name is Elise?"

"No, she's the *woman* Farrah's marrying tonight. Her name is Elise."

"Farrah is marrying a woman."

"Yes."

"Not you."

"No."

"Holy shit. She's a lesbian?"

"Yes."

"No wonder she didn't sleep with me that time I hit on her at the Christmas party. Man, my dick and I are really relieved."

I didn't want to know about him hitting on Farrah, or any woman, or why he was talking about his dick as if it was a person.

"Then why is everyone saying you're marrying her?"

"You know her dad."

Dex growled. "He's an asshole."

"And homophobic."

"Ah. So?"

"Her trust money goes to her when she's married."

"That's stupid," he said. I envisioned him shaking his head at the stupidity.

"He'll find a way to cut her off if he finds out she's gay. The money should be hers, regardless of who she loves. He can't do anything once she's married."

"You're her beard."

"Yes."

"All this time?"

"All this time." I sighed.

"And Bridget?"

"Right person, wrong fucking time."

"Call her."

"I have! Jesus. I've called, texted, emailed. Nothing."

"Okay, calm down." When I growled, he added, "Or don't. It was like, two days and all, but you love her, don't you?"

I tried to explain how I felt to Dex, in a way he'd specifically understand. "If love feels like someone hit you in the chest with a slapshot, then yeah."

41

BRIDGET

I WOKE up when the side of my bed dipped.

"Leave me alone," I mumbled, snuggling into my covers even further.

"Let me ask you something."

It was Mal.

I pushed the pillow out of the way and reached for my glasses.

"What?" It came out as a one-word grumble.

No doubt I had horrible morning breath. If she got a whiff of it, that was her problem, not mine. I wanted to be left alone.

"What do you think your boss–the pervert, I mean–is doing right now?"

That was not a question I expected. I pushed up and leaned against my headboard. "What?"

"What do you think he's doing right now?"

Really?

I pushed my hair out of my face and my fingers got caught on a snarl. It had fallen out of the hair tie yesterday and I hadn't bothered to do anything about it. "It's a little early, but probably at a strip club deciding if he likes a woman's tits or ass better."

She pursed her lips but nodded. "I can see that."

"What's your point?" I asked.

"My point is, he's not thinking of you. At all. Same goes for Professor Dipshit. They got what they wanted and moved on."

Depressing, much? "Is this a motivational speech, because it's not really making me feel all that great."

"If Maverick James is going to be lumped in with those two assholes, then he's not thinking of you either."

"Mal," I groaned, dragging her name out into five or six syllables. "So not helping."

She looked me over and wrinkled her nose. "You've been in bed since Sunday. You need to live your life instead of letting them win."

"Professor Diego *did* win," I reminded.

She shook her head. "No, he didn't. He stole some-thing from you, but he didn't win. Not if you don't let him. As for Maverick, it's time to stand up for yourself, not roll over in bed and play dead."

I huffed.

"You're going to go to Denver, go to that wedding and show him what he's missing by marrying Farrah the beauty pageant contestant."

"I'm not going to his wedding," I countered. No way in hell.

She nodded and poked me in the chest with her finger. "Yes, you are. You're going to go there, look gorgeous and keep your chin high. Show him you weren't broken."

"I am. Broken, I mean."

She reached and took my hand. "No, you're not."

I looked at our joined hands. Frowned. "I think I love him."

With a cock of her head, she gave me a sad smile. "I know, sweetie. I've never seen anything like it and I'm really fucking jealous. Except for this mopey shit part." She circled her finger at me. "But you need to do this. For you. Show him what you're made of."

I shook my head. "I'm not that strong," I admitted.

She looked at me with a steady gaze. "Bridget

Beckett, you're the strongest woman I know. You've survived one hundred percent of your bad days."

I sniffed. "Pulling out the math?"

"You know it."

I thought about her words. Mav hurt me. God, it hurt. But I'd only known him for a weekend. That was crazy. A week ago, I didn't know he existed. I could do this.

Couldn't I?

I did want to see his face when he saw me there, to know that while he'd hurt me–how could he not know that–I wasn't broken. I was strong.

I had to admit she was right. Kind of. It was going to suck really bad, but I did want to face him. To stand up to him, look him in the eye, then walk away.

Then cry and eat a few pints of ice cream.

"Fine. But you have to dress me. And do my makeup."

Mallory clapped her hands and was back to her exuberant self.

"She agreed?" Lindy yelled from downstairs, probably listening for Mallory's squeal.

"Yes!" she called. "You find the outfit, I'll grab my makeup. The flight leaves in three hours."

"Lindy bought me a plane ticket?" I asked,

stunned. While I'd been miserable in bed, thankfully, she'd left me alone.

"Unless that smart brain of yours has figured out teleportation, that's the only way you're getting to that wedding on time." She pointed toward the bathroom. "Shower. You stink."

I obeyed as she began to dig around in my closet. Beneath the spray, I was able to drown out Lindy's and Mallory's chatter about the perfect dress.

I wanted to give Mav the proverbial finger and show him what he was missing marrying another woman. I felt petty though. Vindictive.

Maybe I deserved to feel both because of the way he'd played me. Mal and Lindy thought so.

Except somehow, I couldn't do that. I was sad, yes. I'd felt heartbroken for days. Hurt because I'd trusted someone so much in such a short time. Fell for him.

He'd said he felt it too. That he was falling. That he'd been waiting for me.

Me.

I grabbed the soap and started scrubbing.

Then I thought of his brothers. How could they hang with me like they had and know Mav was engaged to another woman? The wedding was today. Not even a week after we ate deli sandwiches and went out to eat. I sat on Mav's lap. Hell, Silas held up my bra as I ran from the house.

They *knew* we were together-ish.

Turning, I got my hair wet and squeezed shampoo into my palm. How could four grown men spend all day Saturday with me knowing one of them was getting married a week later?

Something wasn't right. I had shitty instincts when it came to men. The inability to stand up to them and fight for myself. To tell them to fuck off.

I did exactly what they hoped. Nothing.

Which meant they got away with it and would probably do it again to some other guileless woman.

With Mav, though, he hadn't diminished me. He'd built me up. Maybe that was why I was questioning myself.

Obviously, I hadn't been an easy lay. He could have had any woman in Hunter Valley in his bed. Even my sister would have probably taken him for a ride. Why would he want to work so hard on someone who was far from a sure thing?

If he wanted only sex, why pick Miss Complicated?

I rinsed my hair and considered. Took the analytical approach.

"Come on, Bridge!" Mallory called.

Mav was pissed at Jason when he treated me like

shit. That he had to do because he was CEO. Well, he didn't have to, but it would fuck over his business if he hadn't. He'd sent me a sex quiz of his own. Told me I could sue and take him for a lot of money. That was a shitty business move, telling a woman to seek legal action.

Fucking me, then marrying someone else, would make most scorned women do just that. Seek revenge. Take his money. Mav knew and did it anyway. Either he didn't care about his bank account, his company, his work integrity, or even his role as CEO–since he said the board of directors could vote him out–or he meant it as protection for me as he'd said. Because he had faith that what was between us was real. That the quizzes meant nothing.

Which meant...

"Holy shit."

...I meant something.

I flipped off the water, grabbed a towel and wrapped it around myself.

When I opened the bathroom door, Mallory and Lindy each held a dress up as if debating between the two. I'd never seen either one before so I had to assume Mallory had brought them with her from her own closet in the hopes I'd go along with their revenge seeking plans.

"I believe him," I said.

They stared at me. Blinked.

"That he's getting married?" Lindy asked.

I shook my head, my wet hair dripping down my back. "No. That he's fallen for me."

Mallory gave me a look of pity and concern. "That's what he wants you to believe."

"Exactly. Something's not right about all this. I've been thinking. Finally. I know Mav. The real Mav."

"You knew him for less than three days," Lindy reminded with a huff.

I shrugged my bare, damp shoulder. "Doesn't matter. This doesn't add up. Let me ask you this, Lind."

She nodded, waited.

"If he propositioned you, asked you for a fun time, would you have had a one-night stand with him?"

"Hell, yes." She didn't even take time to think. "Just look at him."

"And I'd do him right after," Mallory added. "I'm sure he has the stamina to handle both of us."

"Exactly. So why me?" I held up my hand. "I'm not putting myself down, but I've got some baggage. Serious baggage. Any guy would go for easy. But he didn't."

Neither said anything because they were considering.

"I'm going there. To Mav. I'm going to confront him. Hear him out."

"What if you're wrong?" Lindy asked, her voice soft.

I shrugged once more. "Then I'll be wrong and feel like shit, but at least I will have stood up for myself like you two wanted. I'll be able to look him in the eye and tell him he's a piece of shit and he hasn't broken me."

Lindy smiled and Mal pumped her fist.

"But he's not a piece of shit," I added. "I think he needs me to believe in him just as he believed in me."

Lindy cocked her head to the side, then raised a daring red dress. "Fine. Go. Look him in the eye. But you're going to look amazing when you do it."

42

MAVERICK

I COULDN'T TAKE it any longer, knowing I'd hurt Bridget. That my baby thought another man let her down. That *I* had. If she wasn't going to answer my calls or emails, I'd go to her. Tell her the truth in person.

I felt like complete dog shit, and I'd seen a bunch of it lately. What kind of man was I hurting his girl like I was. Yes, I could wait until the news and the truth spread, but I wanted her to know from the start. I'd tried. And tried. But not hard enough.

She might hate me, but I had to make it right. I had to try.

I called Bradley. "Did you get that investigator on the professor at MIT? You got his name, right?"

"Yes. You said Bridget's friend mentioned the name Diego. He's on the faculty list. Math department. The investigator is digging in and will get back to me when he's got something."

Since Bridget wasn't going to get retribution for what happened to her at college, I was. There was no way I was going to sit back and let that fucker get away with what he did to my girl. I had the means and the motivation–Bridget's smile and confidence back–to make it happen.

No matter what happened between us, if she never wanted to see me again, I'd see this problem taken care of.

"Good. I need the plane. I'm going back to Hunter Valley."

"I'm sorry, but the plane's not available."

I wanted to throw my phone at the wall. Why was everything so fucking difficult? "What do you mean it's not available? It's *my* plane!"

"Your brother is using it."

"Brother." That didn't narrow it down.

"Dex."

He made over ten million a year playing hockey. He could get his own fucking plane.

"I can't get to Montana? I *need* to get there."

"I can put you on a commercial flight, but you'll have to fly to Bozeman and drive from there."

That would take hours and I had to show my face at the wedding. At least long enough for Farrah's father to believe it was still a go. Longer than it would take for the truth about the wedding to come out in the tabloids. It would, and fast. Bridget would learn the truth, but alone.

I had to tell her. I had to hug her. I had to know I had a chance.

I gritted my teeth, tried to calm my raging heart. "Put on your to-do list this week to buy a plane."

"Sir?"

"Buy me a fucking plane that I don't have to share with my brothers."

I hung up, then did everything I could not to lose my shit.

43

BRIDGET

I OPENED the front door to go to the airport but jumped back when Dex stood right there. His finger was poised over the doorbell.

He scanned my body, then whistled. "Looking good, sis."

I didn't know what he meant by *sis*. I had on the red dress Mal had picked out for me. She and Lindy both said I looked amazing in it, but I was barely thinking about my outfit. Ever since I decided to talk to Mav, to listen to him and discover if there was a different truth, I'd been distracted. Eager. Nervous. Hopeful.

What I wore wasn't going to change whatever he had to say.

His gaze shifted over my shoulder and his entire expression changed. "Hi."

I turned my head. Lindy was right behind me. Her eyes were on Dex.

Dex stepped back from the doorway, but didn't stop staring at Lindy. "Going somewhere?"

"The airport," I said, taking a few steps down the front walk to wait for Lindy and Mallory to come outside and lock up.

"Hey Dex," Mallory told him. He offered her a finger wave, but still didn't look away from Lindy. It was as if his eyes were stuck on her.

"Introduce me, Bridge?" Dex asked.

"That's Lindy, my sister."

"Dex James," he said.

"Your brother's an asshole," she told him, frowning.

"He is, but he's not the one you have to worry about. I'm the one who's going to marry you."

I started to laugh, because Dex liked to joke, but stifled it when he looked as serious as I've ever seen him.

Um, what?

Mallory ran out the door and to my side. "We need to hurry."

"Marry you?" Lindy asked Dex. "I raised one child. I don't need to marry another." Lindy lifted her chin and stared him down.

Dex was much younger than Mav, probably twenty-six or twenty-seven. Closer to my age than his or Lindy's.

Dex was not deterred by her put down and patted his broad chest. Today he had on gym shorts and a t-shirt for his NHL team. "This isn't the body of a child." He leaned toward Lindy. "I'm all man and I'll prove it to you."

She rolled her eyes and sighed. "Whatever. I can't deal with you today. We've got to get Bridge to the airport."

Dex frowned. "Why?"

"I'm going to Mav. To find out the truth."

Dex paused, ran his fingers over his lips. "The truth?"

I nodded. "He... it makes no sense... we–"

"Didn't he call? Try to explain?"

I nodded. "Yeah. A bunch of times but I was too upset. I couldn't listen to the messages. Or read his texts. Or emails, if he sent any. But now, I want to hear it from him."

"Just read them then."

"No way. I want to hear it from him. And if he used me, then I'll give him the finger or knee him in the balls or something."

Dex closed the distance between us and I had to tip my head back to meet his gaze. He's as tall as Mav and probably formidable on the ice. I wasn't afraid of him. He'd shown he was too much of a goofball for that. "Why?" he asked.

"Why do you think it makes no sense?" he asked, instead of deterring me from putting his brother's balls by his tonsils.

"Well, I believe in us."

Dex sighed, his shoulders dropping and he gave me a smile. "Good. We'll take my plane."

"Your plane?" Lindy asked, surprised.

Dex scratched his head, then grinned sheepishly. "Fine, it's Mav's. The company's. But I borrowed it."

"You're taking me to Mav?" I asked him, surprised.

He shook his head. "I'm taking you to the wedding. Why do you think I'm here?"

44

MAVERICK

I COULDN'T KEEP my mother away. The service was being held in the Presidential Suite of the James Hotel in Denver and she was seated in a leather chair in the suite's large living room. The furniture had been pushed back to make space for the bride and... bride to stand before the Justice of the Peace. There were about thirty people present, all invited by Farrah. I'd had no involvement in any of it besides being the pretend groom.

An event planner had been hired to tackle the details: a harpist playing Pachelbel from the corner, a waiter circulating with glasses of champagne, floral arrangements dotting the suite. While to me this was all a ruse, it was Farrah's big day. Regardless of her father, she wanted it to be memorable. I had a feeling it was going to that in more ways than one.

She was in one of the bedrooms–the suite had three–with her fiancée and two bridesmaids.

I also couldn't keep my brothers away. At least Theo and Silas. I had no clue where Dex was. The last time I talked to him, he was still in Hunter Valley. My brothers stood at my side, silent and stoic. I had a feeling if I really was going to marry Farrah, if I got up there ready to say my vows, they might just beat me up and drag me out of here. I hoped they would.

They knew something was up but couldn't figure it out. Especially since Scout was sitting at my feet.

"You brought your dog to your wedding?" Silas asked. He leaned down and gave Scout a pat on the head.

"Dogs are ring bearers all the time," Theo reminded.

"He's not the fucking ring bearer."

When I'd left the house, he'd wanted to come along. So I brought him. He was easy to like, especially this week. He didn't talk. He didn't annoy the shit out of me.

More guests entered the suite, including Farrah's

parents, who were smiling and looked as pleased as any mother and father of the bride could be. They settled onto a love seat beside my mother, who was a decades old friend.

I sighed with relief, knowing that with them here, my job here was done. There was no way her father could change the legalese for her inheritance now. Farrah would marry Elise and live happily ever after.

And me?

I had no idea, but it was finally... FINALLY... time to find out.

"Time to go," I said, leaning toward Silas.

He looked at me like I was drunk. Or crazy. Or both. "What?"

"Go?" Theo added, glancing around.

Scout hopped to his short feet.

I headed toward the door, not stopping until I was in the hallway and Theo grabbed my arm.

"What the fuck is going on?" he asked, running his hand through his fair hair.

I looked to Silas. "I told you. I'm not marrying Farrah."

He pointed over his shoulder to the now-closed door to the suite. "Then who is?"

"Elise Faraday."

They stared at me. And stared some more.

"You're shitting me," Theo said.

I shook my head and strode down the hallway to the bank of elevators. I pushed the down button, then again.

"Farrah is gay?" Silas whispered.

"Obviously, you knew," Theo added.

"Yes."

"Why all this?" Theo asked, waving his arm in the air, indicating the wedding, the suite, the tuxedo.

The elevator doors finally opened, and Scout dashed in first. I wasn't far behind. On our way to the lobby I explained to them about her inheritance and how she'd be cheated out of it solely because her father was a homophobic asshole.

"What are you going to do now?" Silas asked.

The doors slid open. "I'm going to get my girl."

I stepped out into the lobby and had to pause for a group of hotel guests walking past. Once they cleared, I lifted my head, then froze.

Because standing twenty feet away was Bridget.

She looked fucking insane in a red dress with a low neckline and a front slit that hinted at inches of toned thigh.

"Holy fuck," I murmured and went instantly hard.

The second she saw me, her eyes widened. I watched as her shoulders slumped, then she rolled them back and lifted her chin. As if she was ready to face me. To confront me and show me every fucking thing I'd been missing for the past five days.

I was so fucking proud of her that my breath caught.

Several feet behind her, I saw Dex. Hands tucked into his pockets, he glared, but didn't approach. Now I knew why he had the plane. I didn't want to kill him after all. He brought my girl to me.

She gave a small, barely-sure smile, then said hi.

I couldn't hear her, she was too far away, but I could read that one word on her fuck-me red painted lips.

"Hi," I said back.

Silas whistled and I elbowed him in the gut.

"Groveling's best done on your knees," Theo leaned in and murmured.

"So's eating her pussy," Silas added and that earned him another elbow.

"If she stabs you with that stiletto, don't come to my ER."

"We can't just leave Mom up there. I'll go and explain. Take her home," Silas offered.

"Thanks," I told him, not looking away from Bridget.

"I'll take the dog," Theo offered.

With that, they peeled off, Silas back to the elevators, Theo toward the exit with Scout happily trotting at his heels.

I took a step toward Bridget. She took a step toward me.

Closer and closer we got until she was right there in front of me.

"Hi," I said.

"Hi," she whispered back.

I had no idea what to fucking say. I had too much that I was afraid to fuck it all up. Finally, I asked, "What are you doing here?"

Maybe that was the dumbest thing of all because she flinched, then pasted on a smile.

"I came to tell you I believe in us. That, well, maybe there's more here than it seems."

I wanted to reach out. To touch her. To stroke her hair that was long down her back.

My heart thumped, then skipped a beat. She hadn't told me I was an asshole. Or to fuck off and die. Or any of the possibilities I considered all week.

"I called. Texted. Emailed."

With a nod, she said, "I know. I didn't... couldn't listen or read any of it."

"You didn't?" She didn't know the truth, what I'd tried to tell her so many times. "Yet you still came?"

She looked me over in my tuxedo, then stared at my bow tie. "I, um... guess I was wrong and I should congratulate you. On your marriage."

And with that, I melted. My heart literally seeped from my chest.

She came all the way to Denver to tell me that she believed in us and didn't even know the truth. The truth that had been right there for her to read or listen to at any time.

"Oh, baby. You... fuck. So fucking brave."

I pulled my cell from my pocket and pulled up the last thing I sent her. An email. A one question quiz.

"Here. Read this. A one question quiz."

45

BRIDGET

I LOOKED DOWN at the email, saw that Mav sent it to me on Thursday.

I want to be with you and only you because:
    A- I'm in love with you
    B- I'm not marrying Farrah because she's marrying the love of her life
    C- I believe in us
    D- All of the above

I BLINKED BACK TEARS, then read it again. Mav was quiet and still before me. Waiting. The busyness of the hotel lobby swirled around us. Ignored. I took my time, then finally looked up at him. His dark eyes were filled with worry. A touch of hope, too.

"You're not married?" I asked, my throat aching from unshed tears. I'd thought I cried them all out, but I was wrong.

He shook his head and slowly raised his hand to caress my cheek. "I haven't asked the right woman yet."

He meant me.

"What about Farrah?"

Before he could answer, a commotion had Mav pulling me close and seeing what was going on. There, swearing and shouting about a bad marriage, a very angry man cut across the lobby.

He turned back to me and held me close and told me the truth. God, it was like a truth bomb the way he dropped it all on me. How he'd grown up with this Farrah woman, their fathers' asshole-based friendship. Her sexual orientation. Having to hide it. The trust fund. Mav being her escort to events. All of it.

"Last weekend, she tried calling me, but I ignored her," he explained. It seemed he had to make me understand completely. Why he did what he did. "Paid attention only to you."

"If you responded to her, none of this would have happened," I said.

"If you responded *to me,* we could have been together all week," he countered.

His words stung because it had been awful. All these days and we could have been together if I had taken the time to truly think. About us, about what we'd built in such a short time.

"She's been my friend since we were kids and I told her I'd protect her and keep her secret. It wasn't mine to tell."

"You're a *really* good friend," I told him. His loyalty to the woman showed his integrity.

"I wasn't a good friend to you. I left too fast and didn't tell you. I didn't *want* to keep it a secret. I know we were only together for a little while, but I don't need longer to know you're it for me, baby. These past few days of hell proved it."

I did cry because of that, tears sliding down my cheeks. Hope and relief and happiness overflowed as he stroked my hair.

"They sure did," I confirmed.

"What's one plus one?" he asked, leaning down

and whispering it. His nose brushed along my neck and I shivered.

I smiled against my cheek. "Two."

He shook his head and pulled back just enough so his eyes met mine. There was the warmth, the hope. Everything I liked about him in just a glance.

"One." He kissed me, completely and thoroughly, right there in the hotel lobby. "We're definitely one."

When he pulled back, I was breathless. And ridiculously happy.

"I'm really good at math, so you're going to have to prove that answer," I said.

He tugged my hand and pulled me toward the elevator.

"Mav, where are you taking me?"

"Hotel room. I own the place, remember? I'm going to prove it, baby. All night long."

46

BRIDGET

As we rode in the elevator, up, up to some room in Mav's hotel, I studied him. The way he looked in a tuxedo. Insanely handsome in a way that had women looking twice at him in the lobby.

There was an older couple and a woman with a young child with us, so we didn't do more than hold hands.

I tried to process what Mav had shared. The truth of what he did this week.

He was a good friend.

He was honorable.

He was... *nice.*

And, it seemed, he was mine.

The woman and child got off on floor ten.

Mav tugged my hand and pulled me into him. He wrapped an arm around me to hold me close. I rested my head on his chest. I felt his lips on the top of my head and closed my eyes for a moment. He broke Jason's nose. He manhandled his brother. Both times, it had been to defend me. Yet now he was being gentle. Soft, if that would ever be something that defined him.

I knew it and I wouldn't tell anyone.

The doors opened again on fourteen and the older couple exited.

When we were on the move again, alone, he turned and pressed me into the elevator wall. His hand cupped my jaw.

"My quiz said I'd fuck you in front of others."

I hadn't expected him to say that. His voice was dark. Deep. Completely opposite of his hold, which was powerful and potent. Possessive. All the P's. I looked up at him and blinked. Melted a little.

"If that was what you wanted," he added.

I remembered. I remembered every single word.

"I... I don't want that," I admitted. Nothing about the idea of exhibitionism appealed to me, even with Mav.

His dark eyes roved over my face. "Good, because I

won't do it. That's why I'm not kissing you in the elevator. There are cameras and I don't let anyone see what's mine."

I didn't even think of them, but I melted a whole lot more at his protectiveness. No, possessiveness. Which was it?

Both?

The elevator dinged and the doors opened. He took my hand again and led me down a long hallway. Pulling his wallet from his pants pocket, he pressed it against the lock sensor, then tucked it away again after it clicked unlocked.

He held the door for me and I entered first.

"You... you live here?"

The question showed that while I had fallen for him hard and fast, trusted him so much, I didn't even know the basics about him.

"No. This is my suite."

I studied it, took in the opulent living area with views of the Rocky Mountains out the expansive windows. Through an open door I could see the bedroom. I had a queasy feeling about what he used this space for.

"Um... do you use it often?" I asked, my voice a little weak.

Mav was thirty-seven years old. Of course he'd been with women before me. But was this his *fuck pad*?

He shook his head. "No. Never. Well, once when there was an event here and I'd had too much to drink to drive home."

I relaxed and he noticed.

He stalked toward me, walked me backward into the nearest wall.

His gaze pierced mine, then dropped to my mouth. It seemed he couldn't stop staring at it. This close, all I could see, all I could breathe in was him.

"Baby, do I need to spank you for what you're thinking?"

I nodded and replied with breathless anticipation. "Yes. Yes, I think you do."

He growled and studied me for one more brief moment, then grabbed my hip and spun me around, grabbed my wrists and slowly raised my arms so they were by my head.

"You need only what I can give you?" he murmured.

I nodded, pressed my cheek against the cool wall.

"That's right, baby." Holding me there, he leaned in and whispered. "I respect you, but I'm going to fuck you like I don't."

Oh. My. God.

All that melting I'd been doing had my panties drenched. He found that out when his hands slid down my arms, down my sides, down my thighs to the hem of the red dress, then worked their way back up, taking the material with it.

It bunched at my waist and then nothing else happened.

I glanced at Mav over my shoulder to see what was the matter.

He stared intently at my ass. His jaw was clenched, his cheeks flushed. Every line of his body was taut, as if he were about to pounce.

"Baby, you have a thing for lingerie?"

I swallowed hard, nodded. Felt ridiculously powerful because he was looking at me and was so aroused.

"Just pretty bras and panties," I admitted. "I sleep in whatever."

"You won't sleep in anything when you're with me."

That was an order. Or a vow. Or something.

"As for this…" his fingers slid over the lacy edge of the red panties, the ones I wore since they matched the dress. "I'm not sure what I'm going to do knowing you wear these little scraps under your clothes."

I didn't get a chance to answer because his hand came down and spanked me.

With a startled buck, I cried out. His palm only left a small sting behind and I wiggled because I liked his control.

"When I call, you answer. When I text, you respond. When I try to tell you the truth, you listen," he murmured.

I swallowed hard, knowing I could have spared us so much if I hadn't avoided him.

"Yes, Mav."

He spanked me again on the other side, then tugged my panties down so they rested just below the curve of my bottom.

"How hard do I have to fuck you so you'll remember?"

"So hard," I said on a little, breathy moan.

That was it. The end of his control.

He dropped to his knees and nudged my feet wide. A hand banded around my waist and pulled my hips back. Then his mouth was on me.

"Oh my God!" I cried as licked right up my slit and zeroed in on my clit.

My hips rolled back instinctively to give him better access and his hands went to my butt, cupping the spots he'd heated with his palm.

"I missed your taste," he said, his hot breath fanning over my center. "Missed your dripping cunt. My baby's so wet for me."

Fingers slipped over me, then in, nice and deep. I went up on my toes and cried out.

Before I could process, I was spun around, my hair whipping about as my back was against the wall once again. He pushed my panties down and off, then lifted a leg and hooked it over his shoulder. Positioned how he wanted me, he went back to his task of eating my pussy, this time with fingers *and* mouth.

I moaned and rolled my hips into him, wanting more. "That's it. Come all over my face. Get me nice and drenched."

The wall had no purchase so I grabbed Mav's head, tangled my fingers in his hair.

Pulled him into me, directed him on where I wanted his mouth.

"Mav, I need it," I said, watching him between my thighs. I was lost to the pleasure he was pulling from me with every dirty lick.

He didn't stop, but looked up, his dark eyes finding mine.

His fingers curled in that place I hadn't even known existed until he found it last weekend. It was like a pleasure button because whenever he stroked over it, which he did now, it got me right to the brink of coming.

Then he sucked on my clit, did something with his tongue and I came on a scream. A flex of my muscles. A pull on my heel at his back. A hard tug on his hair.

"Good girl," he said after giving me one final lick and standing. "Now you can take my dick."

I leaned against the wall as if I had to hold it up, but he pulled me toward him and kissed me. His mouth and chin were wet and sticky from me. I tasted myself on his tongue. His hands reached behind me and found the zipper at the back of my dress and slid it down with expert and swift skill.

"Yes," I said finally, processing his words slower than an eighties computer. "I need it." I said the same words again because I did. I *needed.* "Now. Please."

He wasn't the only one who couldn't hold back. Mav was wearing way too many clothes. While he looked amazing in his tuxedo, it was hiding his body. I wanted to touch him. Kiss him. Do everything I could to his body. His mouth was on mine, and I pushed at the lapels of his jacket. Without lifting his head, he shrugged it off, then tugged at his bow tie.

Then his hands were on me and my dress was pooled around my feet.

Buttons went every which way when I ripped at his white shirt.

We were breathing, frantic. Wild. I didn't know how long we kissed, but somehow, he'd moved us into the bedroom, and he turned me toward the bed and bent me over it. He leaned over me, setting a hand by my head and pressing into me. I felt every hard, hot inch of him.

A foot kicked my legs wider, but since the bed was so high off the ground, my toes barely touched.

His hand came down on my ass again. "That's for being a little cock tease in those panties, naughty girl."

I clawed at the bedding and tried to catch my breath.

He moved away and I heard the crinkle of a condom wrapper. I watched over my shoulder as he rolled the latex down his hard length. I didn't dare move, not because I was afraid, but because I didn't want to delay him getting inside me.

He reached out and grabbed a pillow from the top of the bed, then lifted me up so it was propped under my hips.

"Mav," I breathed, never having done it in this position before.

He stepped close and I felt his hard thighs against

mine, then his tip at my entrance. "Shh, take my dick like a good girl."

He pushed in, opening me up.

"Mav!" I cried out, this time because he was so big. I'd never done it this way before, and it felt different. He felt bigger and went deeper. "Oh my God. Yes."

He set his hand by my head again as he held himself impossibly deep. My pussy was still clenching and adjusting to taking all of him.

He held still for a second, maybe two, then pulled back. Thrust deep. Again. And again.

I heard him groan, felt him swell inside me.

It was a lot. *He* was a lot. Bottoming out each time.

"Mine."

Thrust.

"Don't doubt."

Thrust.

"All for you."

He shifted, tangling his fingers in my hair and getting a firm hold. My head angled back and I could see us in the mirror over the dresser across the room.

I couldn't believe my face, the desire, the wild need. My butt was elevated, and I watched Mav's hips as he thrust into me. Then there was his torso, the play of his stomach muscles with his movements. His face.

God. His face. His gaze was on where we were

joined. His gaze was narrowed, his mouth open and slick. He was wild. Feral.

And fucking me.

He wasn't being gentle. Wasn't being careful. Possessive, definitely.

His hand came out of my hair and slid down my spine to rest at the base. His thumb settled right over–

"Mav!"

"Shh," he said, soothing, but not stopping. "Not today. I'll take you here sometime soon." He pressed just a little bit and circled gently, completely opposite of how hard he fucked me. "You'll love it." His eyes lifted, met mine in the mirror. "Holy fuck. Look at you."

It was too much. I never thought that ass play would be something I liked. I hadn't been aroused enough to come for another man let alone be hot enough for something like that.

But with Mav, that extra attention had me clenching, had me clawing at the sheets. Made me wild. I loved it. The sensation was insane and I was going to come.

I told him so.

"Good girl," he crooned, then spanked me once with his free hand, then pressed his thumb into me.

That did it. I came on a gaspy breath, my body tensing and clenching around him.

"Fuck. Fuck," he chanted as I milked his dick, wanting it inside me. Needing it.

He thrust deep with a roar, held himself still and I reveled in the feel. I'd never come like that before I could barely catch my breath.

Mav eventually moved, pulled out of me and went to the bathroom. I heard water running. He came back and with a gentle touch, wiped me with a warm washcloth.

"What's the four hundred sixty-three cubed?" he asked, lifting me up and settling us beneath the covers.

"I have no idea," I said, my voice slurred with satisfaction and sleepiness.

"Good. I did it right."

By it, he meant fucking me into forgetting my own name.

He settled on his back and pulled me on top of him, my legs straddling his waist. My head was on his chest and I heard the beat of his heart beneath my ear.

"You're still hard?" I asked.

While he wasn't doing anything about it, I felt him pressing against my center.

"Mmm," he replied. "Always with you. Baby, where are your glasses?"

"Contacts," I replied.

"I think I like the glasses better. And the pencil behind your ear."

I lifted my head, set my chin on the back of my hand.

"You want me to be a nerd?"

With his head on the pillow, his dark eyes held mine.

"I want *you*. Nerdy, sexy. I love it all."

I couldn't help but smile. This big man, who had everything he could ever want–money, a successful career, family, a dog–wanted me.

"Now what?" I asked, my brain returning and with it, reality.

"I fuck you again."

"I mean after," I replied.

"I fuck you again."

I laughed. "Mav."

He flipped us so I was beneath him. He was up on his elbow, head resting against his palm. His free hand began to roam over me again, something he seemed to like to do.

"We go back to Hunter Valley and do our thing."

"Do our thing?" I asked, running my hand through his hair.

"Note the word *our*. That means together. No running."

"No more fake fiancées?" I countered.

"No more Jake Ryans?" he asked.

I had to smile because, God, what insanity.

"You're my Jake Ryan," I assured him.

"That's right, baby. All yours." He was looking into my eyes as he said that.

I twisted my lips to the side. "We've only known each other a few days."

He shrugged. "I want all the days, Bridget. You, me, Scout. All the days."

He lowered his head and kissed me.

I didn't know it was possible to fall so hard, so fast, but it happened. I hadn't been looking, but I'd found him. Or he found me. No manhunt needed. Only an iced coffee and a sex quiz.

I wanted all the days with him too. No more running. It was time to stick and look to the future.

EPILOGUE

DEX

"Did Mav fuck over my sister or not?" Lindy asked, joining me where I watched the doors close on the elevator where her sister and my brother just disappeared.

"Nope," I told her. We stood side by side, but I turned so her shoulder was against my chest. "He's one of the good ones."

She tipped her head back to look up at me. "Wait. You *knew?*" she practically shouted. "We flew all the way here and didn't tell us? I can't believe you made Bridget suffer."

"Shh, sugar, not so loud," I said, resting my hand

on her arm. Her bare arm that was silky soft and warm beneath my touch.

"Don't *sugar* me," she countered, taking a step back.

I sighed, but tried not to smile. The corner of my mouth twitched from the effort.

"But you're so sweet," I countered, although the look she gave me was anything but. "Look. It wasn't my story to tell. She needed to hear it from Mav himself. Don't forget she shut down her phone. Mav emailed and called her multiple times."

She pursed her lips, ones I wanted to kiss so fucking bad. I may have helped Bridget and Mav get together by flying her to Denver, but I had an ulterior motive: to make Lindy Beckett happy.

Because when she opened her front door... Bam!

I'd felt as if I'd been slammed against the boards, had a slapshot to the helmet. Whatever hockey term that had me down for the count because one glimpse of the gorgeous woman and there was no going back.

"Fine, that's reasonable, but can you tell me now? Please?" she prodded while I stared at her blue eyes framed by ridiculously long lashes. Her pert nose and full lips. All of it I studied and memorized as if it was a new offensive pass in a playbook.

While Lindy didn't know, she was going to be mine

and I'd take out anyone who got in my way until she figured that out.

Yeah, I had it bad. Just like Mav with Bridget. Except while I might be into her, having thoughts about forever and babies, Lindy wasn't so thrilled with me. For some reason, she thought I was too young. Too... who the hell knew what?

"Sugar, you ask so nicely. I'll give you anything you want when you beg."

Her mouth dropped open and her cheeks flushed. Yeah, she hadn't missed what I was laying down. The way her eyes flared was proof she wasn't used to a man being a little dominant with her. Or bold.

"They're back together, right?" Mallory interrupted, sidling up to us with a coffee drink in her hand. She stuck the straw in her mouth and took a deep swig. She believed in the love-at-first-spill-of-coffee between her BFF and my brother.

"Dex was just about to tell me why Maverick broke up with Bridge and then she took him back." Lindy crossed her arms over her chest, which only lifted up her lush tits, then somehow looked down her nose at me which was impossible since I was at least six inches taller.

My dick got hard—no, harder—at how fucking

pretty she was, and her attitude. She'd learn soon enough who was in charge.

"You should aim that anger at your future brother-in-law," I told her.

"Future... Maverick and Bridget marry? They've only been together for a week!"

I wasn't thinking of Mav being her brother-in-law because of him marrying Bridget. No, it was because *I* was going to marry *Lindy*.

I was. I totally was.

I took in her pink toenail polish, her tanned legs that were so fucking long I imagined them wrapped around my waist. No, me holding her ankles against my shoulders as I fucked her. I wondered what color panties she had on beneath the flirty hem of her blue sundress because I wanted to take them off with my tee–

"Well?" she prompted.

"Woman, it's been two minutes since they took the elevator," I reminded.

"She didn't knee him in the balls?" Mallory asked.

I winced and stopped myself from reaching down and cupping my own. I needed to tell them what was going on. They'd dealt with a sad Bridget all week. I'd been pissed at Mav until he told me the truth.

So I shared it all with them. Mav being a fake

groom. Every detail with the hotel guests swirling around us.

While Mallory's eyes widened as I spoke, Lindy barely blinked.

"That was... a good thing he did," Lindy admitted when I was done.

Mallory's shoulders slumped. "God, imagine if Bridge hadn't given you her phone and ignored Mav," she said, glancing at Lindy.

They'd still be in a bed fucking like rabbits right now. Maybe not in Denver...

"That's so romantic" Mallory said on a sigh.

"Our work here is done. I think they're going to be awhile. Like, maybe, a few days. Mav will take care of her."

"That's my little sister you're talking about," Lindy snapped.

I rolled my eyes. "I didn't mean it *that* way. Jesus, sugar, you have a dirty mind. I like it." I winked.

Lindy flushed, which was exactly what I wanted. I wanted to see her do that at other times too, like when I got her bare and told her to part her legs to show me her perfect pussy for the first time.

I put her out of her misery by saying, "I'm not all that interested in thinking about my brother's sex life either. Now yours and mine–"

"I have no sex life," Lindy countered. When she realized what she said, she flushed even hotter and quickly added, "With you."

Yet.

I leaned in and whispered in her ear, breathed in her floral scent. "What do you say, sugar, that we get a room and change that?"

I might have made it sound like I was gently flirting, but I was fucking serious. Or serious about fucking.

Her pupils dilated as her eyes roved over my face and settled on my lips.

Oh, she was thinking about it.

I grinned and that snapped her out of it.

"Are you insane? You're way too young. And... no." I'd flustered her and I was enjoying it immensely. "I need to get home."

Mallory's eyes widened as if Lindy said she wanted to take up belly dancing. "Home? We're in Denver! At a beautiful hotel. What's your rush?"

"We don't have a room–" Lindy replied.

"I kinda know the owners and can probably get you–*us*–one," I offered.

"–and I have work to do."

"You have your laptop in your bag," Mallory countered, pointing to the leather cross shoulder bag Lindy carried. "Besides, it's Saturday! Can't you take a *little* break?" She held her hand up with her thumb and finger close together.

I didn't say a word, just listened, watched and learned about Lindy. How she'd spontaneously flown to Colorado and had enough forethought to bring a laptop. That she first thought about work now that the Bridget crisis had passed. That she wasn't thinking a weekend, or even a day in Denver would be cool.

Or a romp in five-star sheets with me would be fun.

Life altering.

"Do you ever wind down?" I asked.

Lindy shifted her gaze to mine and glared. If lasers could shoot from eyeballs, I'd be a pile of ash on the floor.

"I have a *job*. It pays the bills. You wouldn't understand being a James and all." She glanced around the fancy lobby to get her point across.

Sure, I had family money, but I didn't need it. I'd made my own fortune from hard work. Skill. Talent.

"Lind, he's Dex James," Mallory told her.

Lindy stared at Mallory as if she wondered if the drink in her to-go cup was actually coffee and not something stronger.

"I'm well aware he's Dex James," she snapped. "A James trust fund can help anyone *wind down*."

"Um, that's not what I meant," Mallory replied, her eyes flicking between us.

It was obvious that Lindy had no idea I was a famous professional hockey player for the Colorado Silvermines. Number one draft pick right out of college when I was nineteen. Two Stanley Cup wins.

"She's right," I told Mallory. "I'm only Dex James."

I liked Lindy not knowing who I was. She was being honest and bold, which I didn't think she'd be if she knew the truth. The longer she was in the dark about my profession, the longer I knew she wasn't after me for money or fame.

"My millions got you here on a private jet and can also provide stellar lodging," I continued, "so you should be able to wind down with me. At least until tomorrow when we can go back to Hunter Valley."

Mallory fist pumped the air. "Yes! We're staying."

Lindy glared.

"A room for Mallory and a room for you and me, sugar? I can think of lots of ways we can *wind down* together."

Lindy glared some more, then snagged Mallory's drink and left, speed walking across the lobby to who the hell knew where.

I stared at her ass as she went, and so did other men. I gritted my teeth at the flare of jealousy.

"I've known Lindy practically my whole life," Mallory said. "I've never seen her so riled. I swear she doesn't talk to people like that. Well, except for you." Out of the corner of my eye, I saw her glance my way. "Wow. You've got it bad."

"I'm going to marry her."

She gasped. "Seriously?"

Only when Lindy was out of sight did I look to Mallory. "Seriously."

She laughed. "Good luck with that."

"Want to help me pick out a ring?"

Mallory's eyes lit up. "Hell, yes."

Lindy was going to be mine, ring on finger, baby in her belly soon enough. I played to win and I was going to win over Lindy Beckett.

———

Ready for more On A Manhunt?
Read Dex and Lindy's story in Man Candy now!

BONUS CONTENT

Guess what? I've got some bonus content for you! Sign up for my mailing list. There will be special bonus content for some of my books, just for my subscribers. Signing up will let you hear about my next release as soon as it is out, too (and you get a free book...wow!)

As always...thanks for loving my books and the wild ride!

JOIN THE WAGON TRAIN!

If you're on Facebook, please join my closed group, the Wagon Train! Don't miss out on the giveaways and hot cowboys!

https://www.facebook.com/groups/ vanessavalewagontrain/

GET A FREE BOOK!

Join my mailing list to be the first to know of new releases,
free books, special prices and other author giveaways.

http://freeromanceread.com

ALSO BY VANESSA VALE

For the most up-to-date listing of my books:

vanessavalebooks.com

On A Manhunt

Manhunt

Man Candy

Man Cave

The Billion Heirs

Scarred

Flawed

Broken

Alpha Mountain

Hero

Rebel

Warrior

Billionaire Ranch

North

South

East

West

Bachelor Auction

Teach Me The Ropes

Hand Me The Reins

Back In The Saddle

Wolf Ranch

Rough

Wild

Feral

Savage

Fierce

Ruthless

Two Marks

Untamed

Tempted

Desired

Enticed

More Than A Cowboy

Strong & Steady

Rough & Ready

Wild Mountain Men

Mountain Darkness

Mountain Delights

Mountain Desire

Mountain Danger

Grade-A Beefcakes

Sir Loin of Beef

T-Bone

Tri-Tip

Porterhouse

Skirt Steak

Small Town Romance

Montana Fire

Montana Ice

Montana Heat

Montana Wild

Montana Mine

Steele Ranch

Spurred

Wrangled

Tangled

Hitched

Lassoed

Bridgewater County

Ride Me Dirty

Claim Me Hard

Take Me Fast

Hold Me Close

Make Me Yours

Kiss Me Crazy

Mail Order Bride of Slate Springs

A Wanton Woman

A Wild Woman

A Wicked Woman

Bridgewater Ménage

Their Runaway Bride

Their Kidnapped Bride

Their Wayward Bride

Their Captivated Bride

Their Treasured Bride

Their Christmas Bride

Their Reluctant Bride

Their Stolen Bride

Their Brazen Bride

Their Rebellious Bride

Their Reckless Bride

Bridgewater Brides World

Lenox Ranch Cowboys

Cowboys & Kisses

Spurs & Satin

Reins & Ribbons

Brands & Bows

Lassos & Lace

Montana Men

ABOUT VANESSA VALE

A USA Today bestseller, Vanessa Vale writes tempting romance with unapologetic bad boys who don't just fall in love, they fall hard. Her books have sold over one million copies. She lives in the American West where she's always finding inspiration for her next story. While she's not as skilled at social media as her kids, she loves to interact with readers.

vanessavaleauthor.com

facebook.com/vanessavaleauthor

instagram.com/vanessa_vale_author

amazon.com/Vanessa-Vale/e/B00PGB3AXC

bookbub.com/profile/vanessa-vale

tiktok.com/@vanessavaleauthor

Printed in Great Britain
by Amazon

26157212R10192